Dedication

Thanks to my talented author friend, Tina McCright, who always comes through for me.

Recipe for Love
Night Life Book Three
Dani Petrone

Print ISBNs
Amazon print 9780228638742
Ingram Spark 9780228638636
Barnes and Noble 9780228638797
BWL Print 9780228638780

BWL Publishing Inc.

Books we love to write …
Authors around the world.

http://bwlpublishing.ca

Table of Contents

Chapter 1

Music blared from the entrance of Lazy Jake's Bar and Grill as Scarlett Collins and her friend, Rayna, crossed the gravel parking lot. The night was alive with laughter and the crack of distant fireworks. The Fourth of July in Cave Creek, Arizona, always meant a party. Then again, almost every weekend at Lazy Jake's, there was a party. Tonight just had the added fireworks show and a crowd twice as rowdy.

"We haven't been here in forever," Scarlett said as they climbed the wide wooden steps to the entrance, the boards creaking under the heels of their Western boots.

"I hope they still have hot cowboys." Rayna tugged the heavy door open, then added, "And they're buying the drinks. I spent my paycheck at the salon today."

"Worth it. I love the purple," Scarlett said, stepping inside. "And don't worry, I've got us covered."

"Thanks. I was tired of the pink," Rayna replied. Her short platinum hair, usually tipped in pink, was now streaked with a deep shade of violet.

Scarlett smiled. She was really looking forward to a night of laughs and margaritas. Since leaving her office job to chase her dream of becoming an Event Director, her life had been a blur of clients and spreadsheets. Was event planning exciting? Oh, definitely. Still, she wondered if she'd traded stability for chaos...and maybe a touch of loneliness.

The air in Lazy Jake's hit them like a wall, warm, loud, and thick with the smell of beer, grilled steaks, and perfume. Neon lights glowed over the bar, flickering against walls lined with license plates and faded rodeo posters.

They wove through the crush of bodies, the floor vibrating beneath their feet with each beat of the music. Scarlett spotted two empty stools at the far end of the horseshoe bar. She grabbed Rayna's arm. "Over there. Hurry before someone else takes them."

They slipped onto the stools just as the band broke into a familiar country tune, the singer's drawl pulling cheers from the dance floor. The bartender, a woman with a messy ponytail and a bright smile, appeared and placed napkins in front of them. "Howdy, ladies. What can I get you?"

"Margaritas on the rocks, both with salt," Scarlett said, then glanced at Rayna for approval.

Rayna nodded. "Perfect."

The bartender smiled. "Coming right up." Then she quickly headed toward a guy who'd taken a seat at the other end of the bar.

Scarlett exhaled and leaned back as the music pulsed through the room. It felt good to be out again. Not long ago, she and her three best friends since college had made girls' night a weekly ritual, but life changes. Now, between work deadlines and everyone's busy lives, those nights were rare. Rebecca was married and too pregnant to waddle anywhere but the couch, and Trisha, also now married, was out of town visiting her in-laws. That left just her and Rayna, which honestly wasn't a bad thing. Rayna had enough personality, sparkle, and questionable advice to make up for the other two.

"The last time we were here, Rebecca wore that red wig," Rayna said with a laugh. "And Trisha rode the mechanical bull. Remember how she tried to look classy while crawling on her hands and knees after falling off."

"Oh my God. And how sick she got on tequila and threw up in the parking lot," Scarlett added, laughing so hard she had to grab a napkin and blot her eyes so her mascara wouldn't smudge.

"Right, and you met David," Rayna almost yelled to be heard over the thrum of a bass guitar.

Scarlett groaned. "Don't remind me."

David. She'd actually thought he was *the one*. Smart, funny, handsome, the perfect package. Until he opened his mouth, the truth was he'd always been a jerk. She'd been too blinded by love to notice the warning signs.

When she told him about her dream of planning events, he laughed. Said she should get a *real* job. One with benefits and a future. Or better yet, just marry him and throw cocktail parties for his friends.

She'd shown him the door. A week later, the jerk was engaged. Seriously. The man had a fiancée on the side. Or maybe *she* had been the one on standby. Either way, good riddance.

The bartender returned with their drinks, interrupting her thoughts. Smiling, she thanked her and handed her a twenty-dollar bill. Then, picking up her drink, she turned to Rayna. "Cheers, girl."

"Here's to a great night," Rayna added.

Smiling, they clinked glasses. The first sip was cold, tart, perfect.

Then the crowd shifted.

A familiar laugh cut through the noise. Low, confident, a sound she'd once known too well. Her stomach tightened. She had to be wrong.

But she wasn't.

David stood near the opposite end of the bar, a beer in hand, his arm draped casually around a woman with perfect, beach-waved blonde hair. He still had that charming, too-sure laugh, the kind that had drawn her in before she knew better.

Scarlett froze, fingers gripping her glass. "Dang it!"

Rayna followed her gaze, then muttered, "Oh, no. Is that—"

"Don't say that skunk's name," Scarlett hissed. She lowered her eyes to the rim of her drink. "If I don't look up, maybe he won't notice me."

Rayna smirked. "That man's not worth the calories in these margaritas."

"Agreed," Scarlett whispered. She took a long drink, trying to calm her racing pulse. The music thumped harder, and the crowd seemed to be closing in around her. She turned slightly, pretending to study the drink menu tacked to the wall.

"Scarlett." Rayna leaned closer, her voice playful. "You look really hot tonight. You sure you don't want him to see what he's missing?"

Scarlett shot her a look. "Nope." She leaned slightly to see if his back was still to her.

Suddenly, David turned. His gaze swept the room and landed on her. Recognition flickered in his eyes, followed by that same crooked smile that had once made her weak.

Scarlett's heart dropped straight to her boots. Her stomach clenched as David started toward her, that familiar smirk widening with every step.

"Oh crap. He's coming this way."

Rayna's eyes widened. "Want me to throw my drink on him?"

Scarlett gave a tight laugh. "Tempting idea."

Before she could decide between hiding in the restroom or diving under the bar, a deep voice cut in beside her.

"Sorry, I'm late, Sweetheart."

She turned. A pair of eyes the color of dark coffee met her gaze. His mouth quirked in the faintest hint of a smile, and for a beat, Scarlett forgot how to breathe. All she could do was stare at the tall man with the broad shoulders and tanned skin. His hair was long and almost black, tied back in a ponytail. Holy crap, he was drop-dead gorgeous.

He leaned one arm casually on the back of her stool, the other rested on the bar like he'd been there all along. "Hope you didn't start the party without me."

It took half a second to realize he was pretending to know her, and half a second to decide to play along. Scarlett tilted her chin and smiled. "You're right on time," she said, matching his easy tone.

Rayna blinked but caught on fast, taking a long sip of her drink to hide her grin.

David's stride faltered. He hesitated a few feet away, his expression shifting from confident to uncertain. His gaze darted between Scarlett and the man standing at her side.

"Everything okay here?" David asked, his voice calm but edged with quiet authority.

Scarlett nodded, her heart hammering in gratitude, along with something else she couldn't quite name. "Perfectly fine. I'm with a friend."

"Yeah, David. She's with a friend." Rayna said, emphasizing the word 'friend'.

David muttered something, then turned away, his stride clipped with noticeable annoyance.

Only when he'd disappeared into the crowd on the other side of the bar, Scarlett allowed herself a slow exhale.

"Wow," she said, glancing up at her rescuer. "You have excellent timing."

He smiled then, slow and genuine. "Glad I could help."

The band started another song. This time, their rendition of a Luke Combs love song. The dark-haired man extended his hand. "I think they're playing our song."

"We have a song?"

"Tonight we do."

She hesitated and glanced toward Rayna.

Her friend grinned, then nodded.

Well, I came here to have fun. She smiled, then slipped her hand into his and followed him onto the dance floor.

"You realize I don't know you," she said as he pulled her close to him.

"That's all right," he murmured, his hand settling at the small of her back. "Pretend you do."

Her breath hitched.

Heat radiated through the spot where his palm rested, steady and sure, grounding her in the chaos around them. Scarlett should've pulled away, asked his name, made a quick escape, but she didn't. Instead, she leaned in, matching her steps to his, breathing in the faint scent of his cologne.

Sensible could wait. Tonight, she wanted to feel alive.

* * *

Dante Rivera guided the pretty brunette into an easy, unhurried, natural rhythm. His hand found the small of her back, the warmth of her body beneath his palm. Everything else, the laughter, the shuffle of boots, the clatter of glasses fell away. All he could focus on was the music and the woman in his arms.

He'd noticed her the moment she and her friend claimed two stools at the bar. She had one of those smiles that could light up a room, and apparently a laugh that could turn heads—his did. Dark wavy hair brushed her shoulders, and she looked effortlessly put together in snug-fitting jeans and a white tank top. She made casual look truly good.

He was ready to send a drink over to them when he overheard some of their conversation about an unwanted guy approaching. That was his opening. He decided to play hero for the night.

"You're a good dancer," she said, interrupting his thoughts.

"You make it easy." The words came out smooth, but he meant them. The way she looked at him, as if she wanted to believe him, sent a flicker of heat low in his chest.

"Smooth talker," she teased.

He grinned. "Only when it works."

He couldn't remember the last time dancing had felt this comfortable. Something more than just a way to pick up a woman.

When the music faded, he whispered near her ear, "Thank you for the dance."

"You're welcome." She met his gaze. "And thanks again for the rescue."

He gave her a grin. "Anytime."

As they walked back toward the bar, his arm brushed against her back, and he felt her lean slightly into the touch. The scent of her perfume, vanilla blended with something floral, mixed with the tang of beer and barbecue in the air. He didn't want to let go, but he did.

She slid onto her stool, crossing one leg over the other, and looked up at him with a soft, uncertain smile. Dante caught the faint tremor of her breath and wondered what her story was, why she'd looked so relieved when he'd stepped in, and who the guy was that had her flustered.

He tipped his chin toward her empty glass. "Looks like you could use another."

Catching the bartender's eye, he ordered with easy confidence. "A drink for both of the ladies. Whiskey neat for me."

He rested his elbow on the bar, letting his gaze linger on her. She was lovely. Clear complexion, sensuous pout on her red lips, and shapely long legs, encased in tight jeans that seemed to go on forever. Suddenly, an unprompted image hit him. He pictured her legs wrapped around him as he squeezed that round bottom of hers.

He drew in a breath. The Fourth of July crowd was loud and restless, but for Dante, it all faded into the background. He couldn't remember the last time a woman had caught his attention this completely, and suddenly he wanted to know everything about her.

Her friend with purple in her hair stood, momentarily drawing his focus. She smoothed her short denim skirt. "I see someone I know. Be right back."

They both nodded to her.

When she left, he turned back to the woman beside him, a smile tugging at his mouth. The air between them shifted. Quiter, more focused. He leaned in a little. "Guess it's just us now."

A grin curved the corners of her pretty mouth. "Yeah, alone. Unless you count all the two hundred people in here."

He chuckled. Sassy and funny. He liked that. "So, who's the guy you were avoiding?"

Her expression wavered, a shadow of irritation crossing her face before she sighed. "A jerk I had the bad judgment to date."

"Figured it was something like that."

Before she could add more, the bartender arrived with two margaritas and a whiskey. He picked up his glass and lifted it toward her. "To new acquaintances. I'm Dante, by the way. And you are?"

"Scarlett."

"Pretty name." He smiled. "To new friends, Scarlett."

Their glasses clinked. She took a sip of her drink, and he watched the faint flush on her cheeks deepen as the ice rattled softly in the glass.

"You always go around rescuing women you've never met?" she asked, her tone carrying that same spark of curiosity that had been there on the dance floor.

"Only the ones who look like they could use a little saving." He let a grin pull at the corner of his mouth. "Maybe I just wanted an excuse."

He reached for her hand, testing the waters, and felt her fingers slide against his, tentative at first, then sure. Her thumb brushed over his knuckles, and something low in his chest tightened.

She didn't need rescuing. That much was clear. But hell, if he didn't want to keep standing there, pretending she did.

Her friend returned. Immediately, she noticed the fresh drink. Glancing at him, she said, "Is this from you?"

He nodded. "My pleasure."

"Thank you. I'm Rayna. Her best friend," she tilted her head toward Scarlett.

The three of them spent the next hour talking and laughing, and he found himself having a good time. When he walked into Lazy Jake's, it was just to grab a drink and check out the local scene. A bit of research, technically. He'd be opening a new restaurant soon, just a few blocks away. Different crowd, different menu—definitely no cowboy beans—but still, he was sizing up the competition.

A sudden loud pop was heard from outside.

"Fireworks are starting," Scarlett said.

"Perfect timing. It was getting hot in here." He tossed a few bills onto the bar. "Would you ladies like to step outside and watch the show?"

Scarlett nodded.

Rayna waved them away. "You two go ahead. I'll hold the fort and guard your seats."

Dante flashed a grin and gestured toward the door. "After you."

Outside, the night hit them in a rush of heat. The air still carried the day's desert warmth, laced with the faint scent of mesquite and beer. Laughter and music drifted from the open door behind them, fading into the hum of cicadas and the crackle of fireworks overhead.

Scarlett brushed her hair off her neck, glancing up at the sky. "Still hot," she said.

"July in Arizona," Dante replied. "Doesn't seem to cool down much."

She shot him a sidelong look, raising a curious brow. "Does that go for you, too?"

Giving her a wolfish look, he answered, "You'll have to find out."

For a moment, the world seemed to shrink to just the space between them.

"Come on," he said, nodding toward the edge of the lot. "You'll see them better from over there."

They wandered to the far end of the gravel lot, to where his rental car was parked. Scarlett leaned back against it, eyes lifted to the sky.

"This is better," she said softly.

"Yeah," he murmured, though he wasn't watching the fireworks anymore.

Her gaze met his. "You're missing the show."

"I don't think I am. You look nice tonight."

Another firework burst overhead, washing her in color. Without thinking, he stepped closer, close enough to catch the vanilla in her hair and the quick rise of her breath.

When she didn't move away, he reached out and touched the side of her face, his thumb lingering near her jaw. "You're a beautiful woman. I'd like to kiss you."

"Why don't you?" she whispered.

That was all the invitation he needed.

He brushed his lips over hers, slowly at first, then the kiss deepened. Her lips moved against his with a kind of hungry softness that stole the air right out of his lungs. He could taste the faint tartness of the margarita, mixed with the heat of her breath.

Her hands slid up his chest, fingers curling into the fabric of his shirt. When he pulled her closer, her body fit against his like she'd been made for that space. Every nerve lit up. Every thought scattered.

He pushed up her top. Damn. She wasn't wearing a bra. His pulse skipped a few beats. His finger danced across her midriff, and she sighed audibly.

He hadn't meant for it to go this far. A dance, a drink, a little flirting, sure. But now? He couldn't remember why that had ever been enough.

Her lips brushed along his jaw, a whisper of heat that sent his pulse stuttering.

"We should probably stop," she breathed, though her tone didn't sound convinced.

"Probably," he murmured, his thumb tracing the curve of her throat. "We could go back inside. Another dance. Pretend none of this happened."

She gave a soft, breathy laugh. "Not tonight."

Something in her voice undid him. The world tilted. The heat, the fireworks, and the feel of her pressed close. She was wild and unexpected, and for the moment, he didn't care who might see.

He caught her waist, drawing her in, and she met him halfway, her mouth finding his in a kiss that was equal parts hunger and surrender. The taste of her, salt, lime, something reckless, made the rest of the world dissolve.

Then, another pop, pop, crackle lit the sky.

Voices. Laughter. Footsteps.

"Oh my God," she whispered, breath trembling.

Dante glanced over his shoulder. People spilled from Lazy Jake's, heading outside for the show. He turned, shielding her from view as the group grew closer. For a moment, they stayed frozen, her heartbeat pounding against his chest, her breath uneven against his neck.

He loosened his hold but didn't step away. Her head still resting against him, then she straightened, smoothing her hair, her expression unreadable.

"I'm sorry, Dante," she said softly. "This shouldn't have happened."

He searched her face. "You don't have to be sorry."

But she was already shaking her head, stepping away. "I have to go.

"Scarlett. Wait—"

She turned and ran toward the glow of the bar's open doors, soon disappearing among the crowd of fireworks watchers.

Dante stood there, the night pressing close, thick with the scent of her perfume and smoke from the fireworks. He wanted to call her back, ask her to stay, but the words jammed in his throat.

Part of him thought this was how it was meant to end. Over suddenly, unfinished, impossible to forget.

A few minutes later, he found himself back at the bar, nursing another drink. Scarlett and her friend were nowhere to be seen. The bartender was wiping down the counter, the crowd thinning as the night wound down.

Tomorrow morning, he'd be on a flight back to New York. His business dealings in Arizona were completed. He'd return in September to open another one of his family's restaurants, and by then Scarlett and this night would be a distant memory.

Still, as he stared into the amber swirl of his whiskey, all he could think about was the taste of her kiss and the way she'd said his name. He'd probably never see her again. But damn if part of him didn't already wish he would.

Chapter 2

The blast of September warmth hit Dante Rivera the moment the sliding doors parted, and he walked out of Sky Harbor International Airport. He adjusted the travel bag on his shoulder, then checked his phone for the location of the Uber ride he'd requested just as a dark-blue SUV pulled into the pickup lane. Offering the driver a nod, he stepped off the curb and into the Arizona sunshine. When the vehicle's trunk popped open, he tossed in his bag, slammed it shut, and slid into the back seat.

Within minutes, he was enroute to his father's recently acquired restaurant. This one was located in the small town of Cave Creek. The desert town was a far cry from Manhattan's noise and glass, where he'd trained at the Culinary Institute of America and survived the grind of New York's unforgiving kitchens. But he never shied away from heat, only from failure. And this time, both were waiting for him.

The landscape blurred past in waves of traffic, buildings, and Palo Verde trees, finally giving way to open desert and distant mountains. He leaned back in the comfortable leather seat, took a deep breath, and let his thoughts drift to the reason he was back in Arizona for the second time.

Two months ago, he'd stood in this same heat, signing papers and shaking hands, full of cautious optimism. Now came the hard part. Turn his father's investment into something that could stand on its own. If he pulled it off, he'd finally earn the backing to open his own restaurant, his own vision, on his own terms.

Dante's dream was to follow in his father's footsteps and build on his legacy. As a kid, he'd watched his father turn the Rivera name into one of the most respected in the restaurant world, a brand synonymous with excellence and influence. Now it was his turn.

Just after one o'clock, his ride stopped in front of the new building. Dante thanked the driver, grabbed his bag, and headed for the entrance. The instant he pulled open the glass door, a whoosh of cold air greeted him, followed by the smell of fresh paint, sawdust, and the faint bite of varnish. Beneath it ran a cleaner scent, sharp and chemical, proof that the final polish had just gone down.

He paused at the bar, taking it all in. The counters gleamed under the soft glow of pendant lights, and the leather on the new stools still had that raw, earthy smell of being fresh out of the box.

Out of habit, he ran a hand along the edge of the mesquite bar top, the surface smooth and cool beneath his palm. In a few weeks, it would smell completely different. Garlic butter, grilled steak, citrus from freshly cut limes, maybe a splash of whiskey here and there.

He exhaled slowly. He'd spent months pulling this project together. Late nights, impossible deadlines, and more than one fight with his father about cost overruns. But standing here, he couldn't deny it. *Eclipse Lounge* was beautiful.

And if it all went right, his life would change forever.

A tall, dark-haired man in his mid-thirties walked from the kitchen, recognition lighting his face. "Dante! I heard you'd be in today."

"Hey, Joe. I came straight from the airport."

Joe was twenty-five when he first began working for Mr. Rivera. His personality and people skills made him a natural behind the bar. When Dante heard Joe was relocating to Arizona, he knew he'd struck gold. Joe had a way of bringing a place to life.

"So," Joe said, gripping Dante's hand with a grin, "think we can hold our own against all the cowboy bars around here?"

Dante shrugged. "That's my plan." He dropped his travel bag behind the bar. "Show me the kitchen."

Stainless steel. Spotless lines. Perfect. "It'll look better with heat on the burners," he said, already picturing his crew, his recipes, the rush of tickets waiting to be filled.

Back at the bar, Joe leaned in. "So, what are your ideas?"

"Menu first. Fresh, local. Cocktails that actually pair with the food. Maybe live music on weekends, themed nights to keep it moving." Dante's grin was quick. "If we're doing this, we're doing it right."

Joe smirked. "Coming in hot."

"Wouldn't be fun otherwise."

The next couple of hours flew by, conversation, note-taking, ideas spilling faster than he could write them down. Dante checked the stockroom, tested the kitchen flow, and paced the floor.

By late afternoon, he finally had a moment to breathe. Sitting at the bar with a glass of sparkling water, Dante looked over the empty dining area. In his mind, he imagined it alive with laughter, glasses clinking, and the soft hum of music drifting through the air.

His phone buzzed, pulling him back to the present. A quick look showed it was his dad. "Hey, Dad."

"I'm checking to see if you arrived yet?"

A confident smirk stretched his lips. "I'm sitting at the hottest spot in Cave Creek."

His father's laugh boomed through the line. "I love your confidence, son."

"I learned from the best."

"I want to give you a heads up. I've hired an event planner to help with your opening.

They're sending someone over this afternoon."

"Interesting. I suppose I can use all the help I can get."

"I won't keep you. We'll talk soon."

The moment they ended the call, a surge of determination filled his chest. It wasn't just about running a restaurant and bar; it was proving himself to his father and anyone who'd ever doubted him. He knew the road ahead wouldn't be easy, but that only motivated him more. He would make it happen. He had no other option.

He picked up a pen and a notebook and stepped behind the bar. With an expert eye, he examined the whiskey selection, carefully noting the labels, then moved over to the wine shelf. His jaw tightened. Not a single decent bottle. Unacceptable.

He quickly jotted down a reminder to call the distributors.

"Hello. Is Mr. Rivera around?" a female voice sliced through his musing.

Dante turned, ready with a polite answer, to see a woman walking toward him. Tall, shapely, and somehow slightly...familiar. She reached the bar and slid onto a stool. His eyes widened. Was his tired mind playing tricks?

Scarlett?

Two months since that Fourth of July night. He'd told himself it was a one-night spark, nothing more. But here she was, perched on a barstool like she owned the room.

Large hoop earrings caught the light, sparkling gold as she glanced around. Dark, glossy hair fell in the same loose curls he remembered brushing against his cheek. He could almost feel the heat of her skin again, taste the tequila and summer air on her lips.

His day had just taken one hell of an unexpected turn. A grin tugged at his mouth. Of all the restaurants, in all the towns, she'd walked into his.

And she didn't recognize him...yet.

* * *

Nothing annoyed Scarlett Collins more than someone being late, especially when the meeting could influence her future. Her employer, Gala Elegance, trusted her to plan the launch party for a new venue in Cave Creek. And this was the chance she needed for her coveted promotion. That is, if anyone would ever notice her presence.

"Excuse me." She tapped her fingernails lightly on the bar top. "I have a four-thirty appointment with Mr. Rivera."

She locked eyes with the bartender, and a jolt of déjà vu shot through her. Holy mother of God. She'd know that face anywhere. The dark, intense eyes, the defined jaw line, the easy confidence. His thick hair was shorter now, but it was definitely him. The man she'd danced with at Lazy Jake's. The one she'd been far too forward with after one too many cocktails.

Her stomach dropped. Of all the bars in Arizona, he had to be behind this one.

He moved closer, resting his elbow on the polished counter. "It's that late? I guess time got away from me."

Pretend you don't recognize him, she told herself. Forcing her pulse to slow, she straightened her shoulders and summoned her professional tone. "I'm here to discuss the plans for the grand opening. Can you get Mr. Rivera or a manager for me?"

Then he smiled.

There it was, the magnetic smile that had haunted her since the night she'd been reckless enough to kiss a stranger and think about it far too many times afterward.

"Actually, I'm—"

"Hey, Dante, delivery's here," someone called from the kitchen doorway, cutting him off.

Her stomach plummeted the moment she heard his name. *Dante.* She blinked. Nope, not imagining this; it was him. And now he was looking at her like he already knew exactly what she was thinking.

"Didn't think I'd ever see you again," he said, his voice low, threaded with amusement.

Her throat went dry. "Neither did I." The words came out soft, almost husky. She hated that. Hated that her body remembered more than her pride allowed. "Gala Elegance sent me. I'm the event planner," she said without looking him in the eye.

"Well, now, this is going to be interesting."

Heat rose to her cheeks. "If you're done reminiscing, can you tell me who I should talk to about the grand opening?"

"Sure," he said, voice dropping half an octave. "You'll be working with me. But you might have to remind me how to think straight. You've thrown me off my game."

Don't react. She met his gaze, slow and deliberate. "Then maybe you should work on that before opening night." He studied her for a moment, and she felt warmth slide through her from the intensity of his stare. His lips firmed, and his expression looked serious.

"Oh, I plan to. Making this restaurant successful is important to me." He pushed away from the bar, his movements unhurried, confident. "Come on, I'll show you around."

Scarlett followed, her heels clicking on the tiled floor. As they walked, he told her about the layout and lighting, but she barely heard him. Her mind betrayed her, slipping back to that Fourth of July night. The press of his body against hers. The taste of whiskey on his breath. The slide of his palms against her waist as he pulled her closer, his mouth, oh that mouth. It made her dizzy thinking about it. She inhaled sharply, forcing herself back to the present.

Oh God. How am I supposed to work with him? It's right there in my contract: no personal relationships with clients. One slip and I could lose everything I've worked for. The promotion, my reputation... all of it.

"Everything okay?" Dante asked, glancing over his shoulder.

"Fine," she added too quickly. "Just thinking."

He grinned, the same grin that had undone her two months ago. "Dangerous habit."

She rolled her eyes, but her lips curved despite herself.

I should walk away, keep it professional, pretend I don't notice that look. Who am I kidding? It could melt common sense right off the page.

He stopped suddenly near the expansive windows. Outside, the desert stretched toward the mountains. When he braced one hand on the window frame, he was so close she caught the faint scent of spice and soap.

"This is a nice view. I'll need to add window coverings, but in the evenings we can leave them open," he said, voice low, rough-edged. What do you think?"

"Oh, yes. It's a lovely view of the desert. Especially in the evenings," she managed, her tone brisk, professional, at least that's how it sounded in her head.

He glanced her way with a hint of a grin. "That's what I want. A place that pulls people in and makes them stay."

Her pulse jumped. Is *he talking about the restaurant, or something else?*

She stepped back, needing distance she didn't really want. "It's off to a good start," she said briskly. "You've got potential here."

His gaze swept her face, unreadable now, though the corner of his mouth twitched. "Yeah," he said quietly. "I'm starting to think so, too."

Dante slid a stack of sample boards onto the nearest table. Paint swatches fanned out like cards. "Let's see what you think," he said, his voice lower, slightly softer.

She moved closer. The faint scent of cedar and clean linen clung to him, tangled with something masculine she remembered far too well. She leaned in to look at the samples, and their hands brushed. The contact was barely a touch, but it sparked like a flame to dry tinder. For a heartbeat, neither moved.

A flash of that summer night returned, her body pressed to his chest, his hand sliding up her midriff, his voice against her ear as fireworks lit the sky. She'd told herself it was just the heat of the moment and the tequila. But standing here now, perhaps.... Scarlett forced herself to focus on the boards. "The lighter color works better. It'll brighten the space."

He nodded slowly, as if anchoring himself to the practical. "You've got a good eye."

She managed to smile. "Comes with the job."

He leaned back slightly and seemed to be searching her eyes. "It's really nice seeing you again, Scarlett."

She nodded. "I shouldn't have assumed we'd never cross paths again." Her cheeks warmed. "That night at Lazy Jake's, that wasn't the real me. Somehow, I got caught up in the moment. Can we pretend it never happened?"

Their eyes locked, time stretching between them, one wrong word away from turning dangerous. "If that's what you want." He gave her his sexy grin.

She was the first to step back, her pulse still hammering. "Let's finish the walkthrough of this restaurant. I'd like to see what space I have to work with."

"Right," he said, though the rough edge in his voice said otherwise. "Walkthrough."

They reached the kitchen, and Dante ran a hand along the edge of the prep counter, explaining the upgrades, but Scarlett wasn't listening. She was too aware of how close he was, of the sexy rasp in his voice when he talked.

He paused beside her. "You look like you're somewhere else."

"Just...thinking about logistics," she said, forcing her tone to stay neutral.

"Logistics," he murmured, leaning an inch closer.

Scarlett's pulse fluttered, her professionalism slipping for half a second before she caught it. She stepped away and pulled a small notebook from her bag. "We'll need final menu details before I start advertising."

Dante exhaled, dragging a hand through his hair, the motion drawing her attention more than she wanted it to. His voice shifted, all business again. "I'm interviewing for my team tomorrow morning. I'll have everything you need."

She made a note in her book, then looked it up.

He offered a smile, and something electric passed between them. Scarlett's skin tingled slightly.

"I'm not sure this is a good idea," she said, closing her notebook. "Us working together."

"Why not?" He sounded surprised.

"Because I've worked too hard to let a...situation complicate things."

"Then we'll keep it uncomplicated."

Scarlett's stomach dipped. Easy for him to say. He didn't have a promotion and reputation on the line. Or a heart that still hadn't fully recovered from the last man who'd blurred those lines.

She forced a measured breath and lifted her chin. "Good. Let's make sure it stays that way. Pretend we just met."

But even as the words left her mouth, she wasn't sure who it was she was trying to convince. Him or herself.

"No problem," he answered. "We've already got enough on our plates without overcomplicating things."

Scarlett nodded, grateful for the lifeline back to business.

He chuckled. "You remember how hot the night was, and the fireworks?"

She winced, then turned to study the row of gleaming ovens. "I remember enough." For a second, another image flashed. David was walking straight toward her. Dante pretending to be her date. He hadn't known her name, but he'd come to her rescue. And the look on David's face. Priceless.

She took a breath and straightened her shoulders. "I need this job, Dante. So, can you agree that we keep this a professional arrangement?"

"I'm sorry. You're right. I won't bring it up again."

"Thank you. I will see you in a couple of days with my updates." Without further comment, she turned and briskly walked out the front entrance.

Chapter 3

Two days later, when Scarlett entered the Eclipse Lounge, dinner with Dante wasn't on her to-do list. She just needed his approval for her event proposals. But when he offered another tour of his kitchen and she stepped into the stainless-steel space, the tantalizing smell of food hit. Garlic, butter, and something citrusy.

Suddenly, she was starving.

Her stomach rumbled in agreement. No surprise there. Last night's dinner was a microwaved bowl of soup. Breakfast was a protein bar that tasted like cardboard. The rest of the day, she'd survived on stale office-brewed coffee and a banana well past its prime.

"Smells incredible in here," she said, taking in the scene. Three chefs in crisp white uniforms moved with precision. One flipped chopped vegetables in a sizzling pan, another stirred a large pot, and the third slid a tray from the oven.

He grinned, pride lighting his face, and she had to admit, he looked devilishly handsome and right at home. "This is my team," he said. "They're testing a few dishes I'm adding to the menu."

"If it's half as good as it smells, you'll have customers lining up at the door."

He leaned closer and lowered his voice, "I'm counting on it."

His words near her ear sent an unexpected shiver along her spine. She swallowed hard. "Um, yes." She cleared her throat and added, "Full house every night."

"Hey, would you like to sample the menu?"

"Sure." Her tummy rumbled again in agreement.

"Great. I'd love your opinion."

Before she could answer, he'd grabbed a small white plate from a shelf and was pointing toward a tray of bruschetta.

Her mouth practically watered as he placed a slice of toasted, crusty bread topped with slices of tomato and mozzarella cheese on the plate. Then topped it with fresh basil and a drizzle of balsamic glaze.

He handed it to her. "Take a bite."

She lifted the bruschetta slice delicately, the toasted bread still warm against her fingertips. The crunch gave way, releasing the tang of ripe tomato and the earthy sweetness of basil.

Her eyes widened. "Delicious."

Before she could take a second bite, Dante took the plate and set it on the counter. "Next, try the risotto."

She stepped closer as a chef ladled creamy rice into a bowl and dusted it with freshly grated Parmesan cheese. She tasted a spoonful, savored the silky texture, then nodded approvingly.

"My grandmother's recipe," Dante said, a hint of pride in his voice. "With a tweak or two of my own." He moved past her. "Next is scallops in a lemon butter sauce."

The chef plated them, finishing with a sprinkle of fresh herbs.

He gave her a fork. "Try one."

Scarlett took a bite, closing her eyes as the flavors burst in her mouth. "This is incredible," she said, barely above a whisper. "You're a culinary genius."

Dante's expression softened, a flicker of vulnerability beneath his confidence. "I'm glad you think so. It's not just about the food, though. It's about creating an experience."

"You really are passionate about this, aren't you?" Scarlett looked up at him, feeling a connection she hadn't expected.

"My dream is to open my own restaurant someday. This is just the beginning."

"Well, you've definitely made me a fan."

His eyes lit up. "Then you'll need a proper meal, not just samples." He lifted two plated entrées from the counter. "Come on, let's sit."

Scarlett followed him to a corner table by the window, where he set down the plates and pulled out a chair for her. Instinctively, her creative mind went to work. She pictured white linens, flickering candlelight, and fresh flower arrangements. Opening night would be spectacular.

"I'll be right back," he said.

Moments later, he returned with a bottle of champagne and two flutes. The cork popped, bubbles fizzed, and he slid into the seat across from her. "To new beginnings," he said, raising his glass.

She clinked hers gently against his, forcing a smile while her pulse betrayed her. His gaze lingered, steady and warm, the kind that invited trouble. Gorgeous. Charming. Precisely the type of man her contract warned her about. *A little flirting never hurt anyone,* she told herself, as *long as I remember where the line is.*

"Go ahead," he said, pointing to her food. "Enjoy."

After a few bites, she stated, "I'm not just saying this lightly, Dante. Everything is delicious."

He smiled. "Thank you."

They finished their meal with Scarlett sharing her ideas for the opening. She set her fork beside her empty plate. "Are my suggestions what you have in mind?"

He leaned back in his chair. "I trust your expertise. I know my way around a kitchen, but event planning and décor, not so much." He leaned forward slightly, eyes intent. "I have a feeling you're exactly who I need."

For a second, Scarlett's mind went blank. Was he talking about the job...or something else? Heat crept up her neck. "I'll do my best," she managed, forcing a casual tone. "I was thinking about inviting local artists to display their work. You have plenty of wall space."

His expression softened into approval. "I like it."

"Perfect. I'll reach out and see who's interested."

He pushed his plate aside. "Ready for dessert?"

She had a weakness for sweets and for trouble, apparently. "Absolutely. Bring it on."

He rose, pausing halfway to the kitchen. "You like whipped cream?"

She laughed, flustered. "Doesn't everyone?"

His grin was pure temptation before he walked away. Scarlett watched him go, the muscles beneath his shirt flexing with each step. *Oh, stop it. You're not here for this. You're here to prove you're worthy of a promotion. Forget how reckless you acted on the Fourth of July night.*

She was still lecturing herself when Dante returned, setting a plate in front of her. "Tiramisu," he said. "Fresh whipped cream. Nothing fake."

It looked almost too perfect to touch. But one bite and the incredible, sweet, faintly boozy flavor melted on her tongue. "Oh, my... this is incredible."

His laugh was soft, genuine. "Another of my grandmother's recipes. She made it for my father. One of his favorites."

"I see why he liked it." She took another bite, eyes closing briefly in delight. When she opened them, Dante was watching her a bit too closely. Then he reached out, brushing his thumb across the corner of her mouth.

Her cheeks flamed as she grabbed her napkin. "Sorry."

"Don't be." His voice dropped, almost a murmur. "Nothing sexier than a woman enjoying good food."

Her pulse tripped. The air between them thickened. Until one of the chefs approached to announce they were shutting down the kitchen. Dante rose, thanking him for the meal, his easy professionalism sliding back into place.

"Yes, thank you," Scarlett added, grateful for the interruption—and for the space it gave her to breathe again.

When the last of the kitchen staff disappeared through the swinging doors, the place felt too quiet. Just the low hum of the fridge and Dante stacking plates like some kind of overqualified dishwasher-slash-heartthrob.

Scarlett stood, clutching her notebook like it was armor. "Thanks for dinner," she said, aiming for professional and landing somewhere around breathless.

He grinned in that sexy, confident way he had. "My pleasure. You've got great instincts, Scarlett. I can already tell the opening's going to be a hit."

Compliments shouldn't sound like flirtation, but somehow, out of his mouth, everything did. "Let's just hope the guests agree," she said, trying to ignore the flutter in her stomach.

He walked her to the door, his hand brushing lightly against her back. Totally innocent. Totally distracting.

Outside, the air was cooler—thank heaven. Maybe she could breathe again.

"Drive safe," he said, pausing by the doorway. "Wouldn't want to lose my event planner before she saves my grand opening."

She laughed, grateful for the humor to break the tension. "You mean your secret weapon?"

His grin deepened. "Exactly. And if the food doesn't win them over, maybe I'll have you charm the guests instead."

Scarlett arched a brow. "Nice try, but flirting isn't in my job description."

He held her gaze, a spark of mischief there. "Maybe we should renegotiate that contract."

She rolled her eyes and made for her car before she said something she'd regret.

Professional, Scarlett. Professional.

Still, when she slid behind the wheel, she couldn't wipe the smile off her face. The man was trouble, sweet, infuriating, melt-your-brain trouble.

And if she weren't careful, dessert wouldn't be the only thing she fell for.

"Off limits," Dante muttered as Scarlett's car disappeared from the parking lot. Professional, sure, but those jeans and heels were a lethal combination. The dark blazer and low-cut tee didn't help his concentration either. She was exactly his type, which meant trouble. Big-sized trouble.

He pushed through the back door into the quiet restaurant. Joe was still lining up bottles behind the bar. Dante dropped onto a stool.

"How about a nightcap?" Joe asked.

"Yeah. Jack and soda. Light on the soda." Dante took a sip. "Well, Joe. Think I can convince a cowboy town to trade their boots for loafers."

Joe smiled. "That could be a hard sell, but if anyone can do it, it's you."

"I appreciate the vote of confidence."

"Want me to hang around for a while?"

"No. Thanks, go on home. Spend some time with your family. Once this place gets busy, you might not have the chance."

"See you tomorrow."

"Good night."

Dante swirled the ice in his glass, watching the cubes clink like slow applause.

Arizona. Not exactly the dream. He'd pictured New York—his father's kind of stage—or Paris, where even the baguettes had swagger.

He could still hear his dad's voice. "You want my backing, son? Make the Arizona venue a success. Then I'll finance whatever fancy dream you've got."

At the time, Dante laughed. How hard could it be? Restaurants were in his DNA. But then came the kicker. "Your mother and I talked," his dad had said, which was never good news. "We're not investing while you're treating girlfriends like Uber rides. Prove you're serious."

He'd wanted to argue, but the Italy trip with Maria came to mind. The one that ended in cake, chaos, and a missed flight. He grinned at the memory. The cake had been divine. Maria had been... better.

"Maybe I should give her a call. Wonder if I still have her number," he muttered, then snorted. Yeah. Because what he needed was another distraction in high heels.

Dante finished the last sip of his drink, then rinsed the glass behind the bar, movements slow and deliberate. When everything looked in order, he checked the front door, then headed for the back.

His hand hovered over the light switch. He turned, taking in the polished wood, the clean lines, the quiet hum of potential. The place still smelled new—fresh paint, promise, and maybe a little pressure.

This is my shot. It's not just about making this place work. It's about proving I'm not the screw-up Dad always thought I was.

His jaw tightened. *Maybe I'm still chasing his approval. Or maybe I'm finally proving I don't need it.*

He exhaled, flipped the switch, and stepped into the dark.

Chapter 4

By the next afternoon, Scarlett still hadn't shaken the memory of the first night she'd met Dante at Lazy Jake's. She'd tried focusing on the guest list, flower arrangements, and scheduling marketing posts, but none of it worked. So, when her friends invited her to happy hour, she didn't hesitate. Distraction sounded like salvation.

Now, sitting across from Rebecca, Trisha, and Rayna on the patio of their favorite hangout, the Ritz, she let their energy wrap around her like her favorite throw blanket: warm, familiar, and laced with enough entertainment to make her forget everything else.

Twinkling lights shimmered overhead, fairy dust against the deepening September sky. The smoky aroma of *carne asada* mingled with fresh cilantro and lime, laughter, and the occasional crash of a dropped tray. It had been weeks since they'd all been together, and Scarlett was determined to savor every minute.

Dining at the Ritz on a Tuesday meant tacos and margaritas. Except for Rebecca, who was glowing and happy with her mango iced tea. Pregnant or not, she still looked effortlessly fabulous. Some people just had that gene.

"You girls are spoiling me," Rebecca said, one hand absently smoothing the soft cotton of her maternity dress over her protruding belly.

"Of course we are," Scarlett said, raising her salt-rimmed glass. "That's in the best-friend handbook. Chapter one, subsection tacos."

Trisha laughed. "Especially since you're the first one of us to have a baby. We have to set the bar high right off the bat."

"Please," Rayna said, sipping her margarita. "The only bar I'm setting is the one right in front of me."

They all burst out laughing, drawing a glance from the waiter.

"By the way," Rayna asked, "How'd your appointment go last week? Mick said you were getting an ultrasound."

Rebecca's smile softened. "That husband of mine just can't keep a secret." She patted her tummy. "It was amazing. We heard the heartbeat."

"Aww," Scarlett said, her grin spreading wide. "That's incredible."

"I cried," Rebecca admitted.

"Mick cried too," Trisha added. "He sent us a group text. With emojis."

"Yeah." Rayna snorted. "A crying face and a taco. Classic Mick."

They dissolved into laughter again, the kind that came easily and healed everything it touched.

At least until Rayna asked, "Anything new with either of you?" She glanced between Scarlett and Trisha.

Trisha was quick to reply. "Not much with me. How about you, Scarlett?"

Scarlett smiled. "I do have a lot going on."

"Really," Rayna said, grinning. "Spill it."

Trisha jumped in, eyes bright. "Yes, we want to hear everything. New guy? New project? Both?"

"Actually," Scarlett tilted her head, a slow smile curving her lips. "Both."

Trisha raised her margarita in mock celebration. "Now *this* sounds promising."

"Relax." Scarlett clinked her glass with hers. "No love interest. But it i*s* exciting. I'm planning the grand opening for a new restaurant in Cave Creek."

"Impressive," Rebecca said warmly. "Sounds like a big deal."

"My biggest one yet," Scarlett agreed. "I have full creative control. It's the kind of event that could really move me up at the firm."

"So, who's the new owner?" Rayna asked.

"It's a back East corporation. The guy in charge is the owner's son. Dante Rivera."

"That name sounds familiar."

Scarlett hesitated, caught between honesty and survival. She nodded. "Yes. Dante."

Rayna's mascaraed eyes grew large. "No. Not the Dante from Lazy Jake's"

Trisha blinked. "Wait—what am I missing?"

Rayna's laugh was pure mischief. Fourth of July. Lazy Jake's. Scarlett's mystery man—the one who rescued her from that jerk David. That Dante."

Scarlett groaned, then covered her face with her hands. "What are the odds, huh?"

"About a million to one," Rayna said. "What a night. Fireworks, tequila, and who knows what else in the parking lot."

Trisha gasped. "What happened in the parking lot?"

"It was one kiss," Scarlett said quickly.

"He kissed you!" they all screamed in unison.

"It was months ago. I didn't even know who he was at the time." She picked up her margarita and swirled the straw, trying not to picture Dante's grin.

"Fate clearly did." Rebecca smiled, calm and amused.

"Fate needs to mind its own business," Scarlett muttered. "Anyway, now he's a client, and you all know my company's policy—no personal relationships. Period."

"And how's that working out for you?" Trisha teased.

"Perfectly fine." Scarlett shot her a mock glare. "I'm a professional."

Rayna smirked over the rim of her glass. "Sure. Just keep telling yourself that next time tall, dark, and handsome walks into the room."

"Sounds like we need an invite to the grand opening," Trisha said. "We need to check this guy out."

"I'll make sure you all get invites," Scarlett said. "However, no need to check anything out. Our relationship is strictly platonic."

Rayna waggled a finger, her bright pink polish gleaming under the lights. "Don't act like you don't already have a thing for him. You're terrible at hiding it."

Scarlett laughed, shaking her head. "You're ridiculous."

The server arrived with their food. Tacos, refried beans, Spanish rice, and more corn chips and salsa. It all smelled heavenly. Soon, the subject was changed, and they were back discussing baby names and how delicious the tacos were, but Scarlett's mind wasn't listening. That kiss at Lazy Jake's— the heat, the fireworks bursting overhead had never really left her. She'd told herself it didn't mean anything. It was just a moment in time. But deep down, she realized. Sparks don't go out just because you pretend they do.

* * *

Dante knew she was trouble the second he saw her. Scarlett Collins, walking into his restaurant like she owned the place, confident, polished, impossible to ignore. Then she'd introduced herself as the event planner for the grand opening, and just like that, his focus fractured.

She's off limits, he told himself. He needed to stay sharp, keep his head in the business. Women had a way of complicating things—his father had drilled that lesson in early.

"Get it together, Dante," his father's voice echoed in his mind. "You'll end up like your brother—a loser, working some dead-end job, living paycheck to paycheck."

His brother Dominic was the golden boy. High school football hero, college-bound, his father's pride and joy, until one mistake changed everything. Seventeen, a pregnant girlfriend, a furious father.

"You're throwing your life away!" his father had shouted. "We'll take care of her, but you'll stay in school. You can have it all. Don't ruin your future!"

Twelve-year-old Dante had listened from his bedroom, heart pounding as the shouting turned to silence and the front door slammed. Dominic never came back.

Two decades later, the memory still sat like a stone in his chest. His father's mantra never changed: *Business first. Love later.*

That fear of losing control, of becoming the next cautionary tale, had shaped Dante's entire life. He'd dated casually, avoided entanglements, and convinced himself that emotional distance was discipline.

And then Scarlett walked in.

With her, it wasn't just attraction. It was something heavier, sharper, like a spark hitting dry kindling. She wasn't a distraction; she was a catalyst, stirring up things he didn't have names for. And that scared him more than he wanted to admit.

He raked a hand through his hair and exhaled hard. He couldn't afford to lose focus now, not when everything depended on proving himself to his father. Right now, he needed to prove *he wasn't a reckless kid who let women derail his future.*

If he let himself fall for Scarlett Collins, he risked more than his heart.

He could lose focus on the future he'd spent a lifetime trying to build.

Chapter 5

Dante didn't believe in premonitions, but the dented delivery truck rolling into the parking lot just as the sun cracked the horizon sent a wave of unease slithering down his spine. Two nights of restless sleep hadn't dulled the memory of spending time with Scarlett again. That same charge now twisted into a bone-deep certainty that his day was about to go sideways.

He squinted against the glare, coffee in one hand, clipboard in the other, as the driver climbed out, rubbing his neck like the world had already taken a swing at him.

"Mornin'. You got a delivery for me?"

"Yeah," the delivery guy said as he headed toward the rear of the truck. A few minutes later, he returned, phone pressed to his ear. "Well," he said, lowering it, "seems we've got a bit of a problem."

Dante's pulse quickened. "Define problem."

"There was a mix-up at the distribution center. Your produce order," the driver jerked a thumb toward the truck, "ended up at a hotel in Flagstaff."

He blinked. "Then what's *in* this truck?"

"Bulk pinto beans, forty pounds of iceberg lettuce, and... frozen chicken nuggets."

"You're joking." His grip tightened around the clipboard. This had to be a joke.

"I wish I was." The driver shrugged helplessly.

Dante drew a slow breath through his nose, trying to stay calm. He'd scheduled a training run for his newly hired team. The menu included local greens, heirloom tomatoes, fresh herbs, and every garnish planned to the inch. Now? He had cafeteria food.

"I need my actual order. Can you arrange that, or should I call someone?" This could be straightened out with a simple phone call. Right?

He nodded and reached for his phone. "I'll see what I can do."

"Thanks."

The man disconnected the call, and his expression darkened.

"How soon can you get it here?" Dante asked, trying his best not to overreact.

The driver winced. "Flagstaff's about three hours out—without traffic. Backup crew's rerouting now, but with loading time..." He removed his cap and scratched his head. "Late afternoon, maybe."

"Late afternoon," he repeated, jaw tight. That meant prep time would be rushed, and mistakes would be waiting to happen. He rubbed a hand along his jaw, his father's voice echoing in the back of his mind: *A real chef doesn't blame ingredients—he elevates them.*

It wasn't what he'd planned, but maybe it was what he needed. Opening night was still weeks away. A challenge like this could test his team—and his patience.

"Fine," he said at last, clipped but calm. "Unload it. I'll make it work."

The driver hesitated. "You sure?"

"Unload it," Dante repeated, already turning toward the back door. He needed his team—now. They'd brainstorm, rework recipes, maybe even turn those cursed chicken nuggets into something iconic and unforgettable.

If nothing else, it'd make one hell of an opening-night story.

Inside, the kitchen lights flickered on. Stainless steel gleamed, pristine and waiting. Dante stared at his reflection in the brushed metal and muttered, "Guess it's showtime."

* * *

The smell hit her first. Something fried and suspiciously familiar. Scarlett stopped just inside the kitchen doorway, and a laugh bubbled up inside her. "What on earth...?"

Dante stood at the center of the chaos, sleeves rolled up, clipboard tucked under his arm, and a look on his face that could curdle cream. Around him, the prep cooks hovered uncertainly beside boxes labeled *Frozen Chicken Nuggets Bulk Pack.*

He turned as she entered, jaw tight. "Morning."

She blinked. "Did I miss the memo about Eclipse Lounge turning into a middle school cafeteria?"

He exhaled through his nose, clearly fighting for patience. "Delivery mix-up. My produce orders are currently enjoying the mountain air in Flagstaff."

"Ah," she said, eyeing the stack of boxes. "And in its place, we have... nuggets."

"Apparently so." He gave a humorless smile. "Forty pounds of them."

Scarlett bit back a grin. "Well, on the bright side, I hear kids love finger food."

He shot her a look that was half glare, half surrender. "You're enjoying this."

"Maybe just a little." She stepped closer, inspecting the boxes like a detective at a crime scene. "So, what's your plan? Opening a drive-thru?"

"Working on it." He set the clipboard down with a *thunk*, clearly becoming annoyed by her teasing. "Maybe a rebrand. Turn a disaster into a feature. A gourmet twist on comfort food. Nostalgia meets fine dining. Give them out free to the passerby's."

Scarlett tilted her head, impressed despite herself. "That's actually... not terrible."

"High praise."

"I'm serious," she said, fighting a smile. "It's clever. Play it off as intentional. Something cheeky for the pre-opening crowd. You could call it..." She tapped her chin. "*Nuggets of Innovation.*"

That earned her a laugh—low, genuine, and far too attractive for her sanity.

He looked at her for a beat longer than necessary, amusement flickering in his eyes. "You know," he said softly, "you might be the only person who could make a catastrophe sound marketable."

"Occupational hazard," she replied, straightening. "I sell chaos for a living."

She cleared her throat. "All right. I'll draft a quick post for social media—something playful about your secret test kitchen. We'll lean into the humor."

Dante nodded slowly, the corner of his mouth lifting. "A comedy of errors."

"Can we get through today without a food fight?"

He smiled. "No promises."

Scarlett rolled her eyes, but the corners of her mouth betrayed her. "Go. Save your nuggets, Rivera."

As she turned toward her laptop, he heard him muttering something about culinary redemption. And despite herself, Scarlett couldn't help smiling, too. It wasn't the morning she'd planned. But then again, nothing about Dante Rivera was going according to plan.

She found a corner spot at the bar, settled herself onto a stool, and opened her laptop. She was about to check her emails when an idea sparked. She immediately jumped off the stool and headed to the kitchen. "Dante, I know who might want those nuggets."

He raised his brows.

"Mick. Rebecca's husband." She beamed. "He owns Mo's, a biker bar. They serve wings, fries, and all kinds of bar food. He could use the nuggets. I'm sure he'd love a deal."

Dante blinked, as if the concept of someone *wanting* forty pounds of frozen chicken was brand-new information. "You think he'd actually want them?"

"Mick once tried to sell deep-fried pickles as a diet food. He's your guy."

That earned her a laugh. Low, surprised, genuineness. "You're right. My kinda guy. Let's make it happen."

Within twenty minutes, Rebecca had texted Mick, and a deal was struck. Mo's bar now owned forty pounds of Dante's problem. And the Eclipse Lounge's kitchen looked a lot less tragic.

As the driver Mick had sent, loaded the boxes into his van, Dante leaned against the counter, shaking his head. "You realize you saved my day?"

"Happy to help," Scarlett said, pretending to check her notes. "Though if I were you, I'd ask for naming rights. 'Mo's

Chicken Nuggets à la Eclipse' has a nice ring to it."

He chuckled. "You're wasted in event planning. You could run PR for the apocalypse."

"Thanks, I think."

He hesitated then, that same sexy spark flickering behind his eyes. "Seriously, though. You're good at this."

Scarlett met his gaze. "It's my job to make sure chaos looks intentional."

As she gathered her things, she caught his reflection in the polished metal of the fridge, smiling to himself, just a little. And for the first time that morning, she realized the thought of saving Dante Rivera's day had been... kind of fun.

"Hey," he said as he was about to head out. "If you like, you're welcome to work from here. The restaurant area is quiet. I'll provide food."

Tempting offer, she thought. Hot gourmet lunch or peanut butter at her office? "Thanks. I think I'll take you up on that."

The rest of Scarlett's day disappeared in a blur of marketing updates and social-media scheduling. She managed to contact several artists about showcasing their work and return a dozen calls before Dante served her lunch, along with the news that his first order, which had ended up in Flagstaff, had finally been delivered.

Hours passed before Scarlett decided to call it done for the day. She packed up her things and made her way to the kitchen, where Dante sat with his head buried in a notebook, completely lost in thought.

"Good night, workaholic," she teased.

He looked up. "Thanks again,"

She tilted her head. "For what?"

"Saving the day."

"Glad I could. I'll be back tomorrow. I'll have more ideas for your approval." She gave him a wave and headed out.

By the time Scarlett slid into her car, the late afternoon sun had dipped low enough to turn the sky the color of rose gold. The kind of light that made everything look softer, even a chaotic day involving forty pounds of chicken nuggets.

She rested her hands on the steering wheel, letting out a small laugh. "Nuggets," she muttered, shaking her head. "Who would've thought?"

The truth was, she'd enjoyed herself more than she wanted to admit. Fixing the problem, watching Dante relax for the first time all day, hearing him laugh...it had felt good. Too good.

She should've been thinking about contracts, deadlines, and her upcoming presentation for the promotion. Instead, her mind kept circling back to Dante and the way he'd looked at her like she was more than just the event planner hired to keep his restaurant on track.

Scarlett sighed, starting the engine. "He's your client," she reminded herself. "Nothing more."

But as she pulled out of the parking lot, his laughter lingered, impossible to shake. And for the first time in a long while, she wasn't entirely sure she believed herself.

Chapter 6

By the next morning, yesterday's chaos had faded, replaced by the quiet buzz of planning. Scarlett placed several photos of tall floral centerpieces on the bar countertop.

Dante's brow furrowed. "These look like they belong at a garden party. People should see each other when they're eating, not fight through a jungle."

"They're a focal point, Dante. They draw the eye and create ambiance."

"They also block the view of the food, which, by the way, *is* the focal point."

She exhaled, eyeing him with mock patience. "Fine." She slid another sketch across the counter. "Low arrangements. Soft candles. Elegant and practical."

He studied the photo, then nodded. "Better. But lose the battery-operated candles. This is upscale. I want real candlelight."

"You do realize those are a fire hazard, right? Battery candles have the same effect without the risk."

He gave her a look that said, *Not in my restaurant.*

"Fine," she said with a sigh. "Real candles."

A faint smile tugged at his mouth. "Didn't think you'd compromise so easily."

"Don't get used to it."

Their eyes met briefly. Scarlett looked away first, pretending to straighten the papers on the counter. Her pulse quickened, uninvited memories flickering through her mind: a warm night, a quiet parking lot, and Dante's mouth on hers. One kiss that had meant nothing. Or everything. She still wasn't sure.

Pushing the thought aside, she lifted another photo. "Okay. Lighting. The room's functional but harsh. I'm thinking of uplighting along the walls. Maybe adding some string lights near the bar."

"String lights? What is this, a backyard barbecue?"

"Not those plastic ones, Dante. I mean warm, subtle lighting. It'll make the space feel intimate."

He crossed his arms, ready to object, but the front door opened, and a delivery driver rolled in crates of produce.

"Where do you want these?" the man asked.

"Straight back," Dante pointed toward the kitchen. "Careful around the walls."

When the door swung closed again, Dante turned back. "Look, I appreciate creativity, but my father's built this brand on tradition. I don't want to lose what our diners expect."

Scarlett softened her tone. "I get that. But you hired me to *impress* people. That means stepping outside the familiar, and honestly, no one in Cave Creek knows what to expect. That's your advantage."

Dante pressed his hand to his chest. "Ouch."

"Truth hurts."

Their gazes caught again, challenge meeting amusement, and for a moment, the air between them hummed with unspoken energy.

He sighed and gestured to her vision board. "Fine. Show me more of your grand plan. But if I see anything resembling a disco ball, I'm pulling the plug."

Scarlett arched a brow. "Although..."

"No disco balls."

They both laughed, the tension breaking. As she continued her presentation, Dante's skepticism slowly gave way to curiosity as she outlined her ideas. The longer she talked, the more that invisible boundary between work and something more began to blur.

"All right," she said finally, flipping open her notebook. "Seating. How many can we fit inside comfortably?"

"Eighty. Plus, the bar," he answered, practical as ever.

She frowned. "Not enough. Are you including the patio?"

"We don't have an actual patio area," he said flatly.

Scarlett froze, pencil midair. "Sure you do. That concrete space that wraps around the side of the building."

He shook his head. "That's just a plain slab. I'll extend the roof out to cover it sometime down the road."

"Oh my gosh, Dante. This is Arizona. People *live* for patios."

"Well, I—"

"Don't worry, I'll call a contractor." She was already scrolling through her contacts.

His voice jumped an octave. "A contractor?"

"Yes. We'll make it work. A patio's a must-have." She scribbled the word *'patio'* *under 'urgent tasks'*.

"How much money are we talking about?"

"Details," she said, waving him off. "You'll make it back."

"Scarlett—"

"We'll discuss it," she interrupted sweetly. "After the bids come in." She gathered her sketches and samples, slipping them into her bag. "Oh—and we should decide where to put the firepits and water features."

"Firepits? Water features?" he echoed, his voice an octave higher.

"Must-haves," she said matter-of-factly, smoothing the sleeve of her blouse. "I seem to remember you like it hot."

Her breath caught. *Why did I say that?* Heat crept up her neck. She forced a laugh. "Anyway. See you tomorrow... friend."

She left before he could respond, his stunned expression still etched in her mind. Outside, the lowering sun painted the pavement in gold. She pulled out her phone, dialed her favorite contractor, and wasn't surprised when it went straight to voicemail.

"Of course," she muttered, smiling despite herself.

By the time she reached her apartment, twilight had settled in. She kicked off her heels, dropped her bag, and stood for a moment in the quiet. The silence pressed close, familiar and oddly comforting.

She poured a glass of water, leaning against the kitchen counter, her thoughts chasing one another like loose pages in a breeze. Could she really pull off a new patio in three weeks? Maybe. She'd done crazier things. Her phone buzzed. A group text from Trisha and Rayna.

We need a date for Rebecca's baby shower. How's the project with the hot guy?

Scarlett smiled, typing back:

No idea on the shower. Swamped.

She hit send, then hesitated, her fingers still resting on the screen. She couldn't dump it all on her friends. She'd find a way. She always did.

Because panic didn't belong in her world, she turned chaos into charm, pressure into polish. That was her gift. Her shield.

But as she opened her laptop and the screen lit her face, her mind betrayed her, wandering back to Dante and the way he'd watched her explain her ideas. A flicker of respect behind his skepticism.

It unsettled her. Impressed her. Maybe both.

She exhaled, closing her eyes for a moment. *Stay focused, Scarlett. Just a few weeks. That's all you need to survive and move on.* But as her pulse slowed, a single thought lingered, quiet and dangerous. She wasn't sure she wanted to.

* * *

Dante sighed and slowly ran his fingers through his hair. What was he thinking? How had he let Scarlett add additional expenses to his budget? Did she really believe a patio area would make a big difference?

Trying to distract himself, he reached for his notepad and stared at the menu he'd penciled on the first page. He'd changed it three times over the past two days. Somehow, he couldn't seem to focus. He was starting to doubt himself more and more. Maybe running a place on his own was a bad idea. Hell, maybe he should have kept working in the kitchen at one of his dad's proven restaurants. It'd sure be easier.

He heaved a sigh. Who was he kidding? He never liked to take the easy way. Easy was boring. He knew it was the challenge that fueled his heart. So, one way or another, the Eclipse Lounge would be the 'it' place everyone wanted to experience. After all, he'd already made a promise to his dad and to himself.

Deep in thought, he stared unseeing out the front window. What he needed right now was a hot shower and a good night's sleep. But every time he closed his eyes, he saw a restaurant empty of customers.

Chapter 7

The next morning, Scarlett entered the lounge with coffee in one hand and a vision board in the other. She hadn't slept much, maybe four hours, at most, but she'd pulled herself together.

Sliding onto a barstool, she caught her reflection in the mirror behind the bar. She looked decent. After showering earlier, she slicked her hair into a ponytail and put on her favorite navy-blue blouse and comfortable jeans. Then she pushed her feet into four-inch heels that made her footsteps echo with authority. She didn't come here this morning to play around. She'd come to work.

"Dante?" she called.

No response. She slid off the stool and headed toward the kitchen. He looked up from the prep station, sleeves rolled up, hair slicked back, and looking slightly damp. Two staff members hovered nearby, a sous chef she recognized and a younger guy who looked like he hadn't had coffee yet.

"Morning," Dante said.

Scarlett's gaze flicked to the whiteboard covered with scribbles of menu revisions, timelines, and ingredient substitutions.

He wiped his hands on a towel. "Didn't think you were the early type."

"I'm the *necessary* type," she said coolly, scanning the room. "Any word on the wine pairings?

"Haven't heard a thing," Dante said.

Scarlett frowned. "Perfect. Third strike." She'd given that sommelier more chances than she deserved—and now regretted it.

Dante gave a slow nod. "Want me to say it?"

Scarlett narrowed her eyes. "Say what?"

"You need to hire someone new."

She didn't argue. Of course, he was right. She just hated hearing him say it. "I know," she admitted quietly, "Lesson learned."

Her phone pinged. "The contractor's here."

He gave a low whistle. "You're serious about that thing.

"You told me to go all in."

Something unreadable flickered behind his eyes. "Yeah. I did."

Before either of them could say more, a tall man in a faded flannel shirt and reflective sunglasses entered, a rolled blueprint under one arm.

Scarlett crossed the room to meet him, extending her hand. "Good morning, Rick. Thank you for coming so soon." She turned slightly. "This is Dante Rivera. His father is the owner."

Rick shook Dante's hand. "Nice to meet you. Let's have a look at your idea?"

Outside, Rick surveyed the concrete pad next to the lounge, walking its perimeter and muttering to himself.

Scarlett listened as he explained the permits required and answered his questions about square footage and material preferences.

After fifteen minutes and a few notes on his clipboard, Rick removed his sunglasses and looked at them. "I can possibly do it. Tight window, though. You'll need permits expedited, labor lined up by the weekend. We're talking premium rates to make it happen. And even then, I can't make any promises."

"How premium?" Dante inquired.

Rick's eyebrows raised. "Full job, start to finish, including labor, permits, after-hours work, and custom railing." He paused, then quoted the number.

Scarlett didn't flinch. But she couldn't miss that Dante did.

"That's," he blinked. "That's a bit more than I had in mind."

"Welcome to construction in a hurry," Rick said. "I can knock five percent off if we skip the planter boxes."

"No," Scarlett said instantly. "The planters stay."

Dante crossed his arms. "I need to think about this?"

Rick handed him the written estimate. "I understand. However, there's a lot of rescheduling to accommodate your schedule. I'll need your answer by tomorrow."

When the contractor left, Scarlett turned to Dante. "It's not a big deal. We're only expanding it a few feet and adding a cover. Plus, the firepit and water feature. You did tell me to make this place unforgettable. This patio will help do that."

Dante rubbed the back of his neck. "Unforgettable, huh?"

She let the silence stretch before flashing a smile. "Oh, absolutely."

* * *

Dante stood just outside the back door, his phone pressed to his ear, staring down the empty alley like it might hold a better answer than the one he was about to get.

It rang twice before his father's gravelly voice came on the line. "Yeah?"

"Hey. It's me."

A pause. "You okay?"

"I'm fine," Dante said quickly, too quickly. "I need to run something by you."

"What's going on?"

Dante swallowed hard. "We're adding a patio to the lounge. Scarlett found a guy who might be able to build it in time, but it's not cheap. We'll need to bump the budget."

"Patio? You need a patio?"

"Scarlett says we do." Dante quickly revealed the cost to build it before his dad had a chance to think it over.

A low whistle came through the line, followed by silence.

"What do you think, Dad?"

"That's a hell of a patio."

Dante closed his eyes. "I'm going to give the go-ahead. I hope I have your approval."

Another pause. Finally, he responded, "I told you to spare no expense." He chuckled. "Didn't think you'd take it so literally."

"You said you wanted to make a statement."

"I did. But use good judgment. Make sure the numbers work. We've been running successful businesses without patios for twenty years."

Dante straightened slightly. "This place will be successful," Dante said confidently. I've got one year to prove it."

On the other end, his father exhaled hard. "Just don't drown in your ambition."

The unexpected remark stung.

"I'm a good swimmer," Dante answered. "I'm determined to make the Eclipse Lounge as good or better than any of your other restaurants."

There was a brief pause. Then his father's voice softened—just barely. "Fine. Pull the money from the contingency fund. But no more surprises, Dante. You don't start a business in the red and expect to make a decent profit in the first year,"

"I know," Dante said, his voice tight in his throat.

"Good." His father's tone snapped back to business. "Call me with any updates."

Dante let the phone fall to his side and stared at the wall across the alley. He'd gotten approval for the money, but it didn't feel like a win. He took a breath and let his mind drift back to a different time and place. Manhattan. Dante stood just outside the glass-walled office, palms sweating, a marketing proposal clenched in his hand. He was twenty-three, fresh out of college, and had spent three sleepless nights preparing the pitch. All he needed was a chance. His father sat behind the massive desk, the phone to his ear, his eyes fixed on the computer. The usual: calm, composed, unreadable.

"Dad?" Dante's voice had cracked slightly. He hated that.

His father had held up one finger without looking away, then finished the call. "What is it, son?" he asked, finally glancing up.

"I... I put together an idea," Dante said. "Something different. More interactive. I think it could pull in a younger crowd." He handed over the file.

His father had taken it but didn't open it. "You've been working here what now, one month?"

"Two," Dante said.

His father leaned back in his chair and finally opened the folder. His eyes flicked over the first page, then the second. "It's ambitious."

Dante had nodded, heart pounding. "But effective. I ran projections. If we—"

"I didn't ask for projections," his father said sharply. "I asked for discipline. You don't walk into this business throwing glitter and hoping it sticks."

"It's not glitter," Dante replied, stung. "It's a strategy."

His father stared at him for a long moment, then closed the folder and set it aside. "You want to prove something, son? Show me you can follow instructions before you start rewriting the rules."

"I want to help." He'd forced himself to remain calm.

"I know," his father said. "But this isn't a playground. It's our family business."

Dante shoved his phone into his pocket, his jaw clenched. That day had left its mark on him. His ambition was seen as arrogance. His ideas were dismissed as childish. Feeling hurt, he distanced himself from his family and took a few random jobs that led nowhere. After some serious soul-searching, he returned home. He was welcomed with open arms, and soon, with his father's full support, he enrolled at the Culinary Institute.

Now he had this opportunity. And come hell or high water, he'd make it happen. This time, no one was going to shove his ambition into a drawer. He'd make Eclipse Lounge the most sought-after establishment in his family's chain of restaurants.

He turned and walked through the back door.

Chapter 8

The following morning, Dante slid onto the barstool beside Scarlett, where she sat twirling a strand of dark hair around her finger. "No problem," he said.

"Excuse me?" She glanced up, her brows were knitted slightly.

"The patio. There's no problem." *No problem as long as it pays off.* But that was tomorrow's headache. For now, his attention remained on the brunette beside him and how her hair caught the light, glowing like flames dancing in the fire.

"Perfect," she said, tapping something into her computer. "I'll let Rick know he can start ASAP." She exhaled deeply, as if she was finally allowing herself to breathe.

"Can I get you more coffee? Or make you a drink?"

"No thanks. I'm fine." She reached for the coffee mug. As she stretched, his gaze lingered on the delicate curve of her back; the slight dip drew his focus like a magnet.

He imagined her turning and leaning into him and offering a smile. His breath hitched. He had to get control of his thoughts.

"Sorry if I'm not talkative this morning. I've got a lot of things that need immediate attention. I have to schedule the promo, order more flowers, and decide what we're doing about the music."

"Sounds like a party," he said, leaning closer to get a look at her computer screen.

"Not yet," she replied as her fingers danced across the keyboard. "But it will be. Opening night has to be perfect."

He nodded, even though she wasn't looking at him. "I get it. Just don't forget to breathe."

"I'll breathe after opening night, and the promotion I'm working toward is secured."

"Promotion?"

"You bet. This project will give me the edge I need. I will become a full-fledged Event Director and partner with Gala Elegance."

There it was, that edge, calm and competent. And yet, he saw the faint shadows under her eyes, the way her shoulders tightened when she thought no one was watching. She was holding it all together with steel and grit.

Scarlett turned to face him, one brow raised. "There is something you can do. If you want to help..." She paused, like weighing whether to say more. "That light over table six keeps flickering. It's driving me insane."

Dante blinked. He followed her gaze to the corner. "I noticed that earlier. Thought maybe it was intentional." He gave her a quirky smile. "You know, ambiance."

"It's not," she said, deadpan. "It's broken."

A quiet beat passed between them. Then he nodded, slowly. Obviously, she was in no mood for joking. "I'll grab a ladder."

He retrieved the ladder from the storage closet, carried it into the bar, and set it beneath the flickering light. Scarlett didn't look up, but he caught the subtle shift of her gaze when he climbed the rungs.

"That should do it," he replied, twisting the bulb into place until the flicker stilled. "And for your information, I was the unofficial handyman in my college dorm room. They said I had steady hands."

She didn't answer right away. Then, without looking up from the screen, she murmured, "Good to know."

He laughed softly under his breath and climbed down.

She finally glanced at him. "You're a handy guy."

"That's the nicest thing you've said to me today."

"Don't let it go to your head."

"No promises."

Their eyes locked, heat flickering beneath the easy banter. The room went quiet for a beat before she looked away, then powered down her laptop. "I need that wine list you promised. The one with the custom pairings."

"It's at my place. We can go get it."

She hesitated just long enough for him to notice. Then she shrugged. "Sure. I guess I can do that."

He opened the door for her, but she brushed past first, still in charge. And yet, she was going. Dante followed, heart hammering a little harder than it should.

* * *

Scarlett mentally repeated the same mantra all the way to Dante's house. Only business. Review the wine list. Discuss marketing. That was it. Nothing more. But when she pulled into his driveway and saw him waiting by the door, her heart betrayed her with an undeniable skip, and she knew she was lying to herself.

Stepping out of the car, she let the evening air cool her flushed cheeks. It didn't help. The moment she brushed past him inside, the faint scent of his aftershave caught her off guard, sending a ripple through her chest. She should have told him to email the list. Should've said no the second he flashed that infuriating grin and said it was at his place.

Instead, here she was.

Determined to keep the evening on track, she lifted her chin and forced her voice into a professional calm. "All right. Let's get down to business. Get me your wine list."

He smiled, but his eyes appeared troubled. "Scarlett, about the night at Lazy Jake's. I feel like a jerk."

She'd wondered if he'd bring that night up again, but she wasn't expecting it the minute she walked through the door. "Dante, it happened. It was a mistake. Forget it."

"I can't," he said with sincerity in his voice.

She blew out her breath, dropped her bag onto a chair, and turned to him. "Okay." She crossed her arms. "Get it off your chest so we can move on and get to work."

He cleared his throat. "I took advantage of you. I knew you were upset. The old boyfriend and all. You were drinking. So, I apologize."

"Thank you. Apology accepted." She gave a short nod. "Now, can we put this all behind us and focus on our project?"

"I was worried you'd change your mind and quit this job."

That surprised her. "Quit? Nope, I have no intention of quitting. I'm committed to making your opening night spectacular. I told you what this event means for me."

He looked at her for a moment, then nodded toward the kitchen. "Come on then, I'll get you the wine list."

"Right," she said, then followed him down the hallway, trying not to notice how perfectly his tight jeans hugged his rear end.

Dante flipped the light switch and gestured to her to sit. As the overhead lighting brightened the room, she obediently eased onto a barstool at the kitchen island and watched him open a drawer. With his back to her, she had a clear view of his shoulder muscles stretching under his T-shirt. Trying to distract herself, she drummed her fingers against the smooth surface of the granite countertop.

"Here's the list." He placed a printed-out page in front of her. "They sent over several bottles to sample."

"And you brought them home instead of leaving them at the bar?"

"I guess I hoped some lovely lady would stop by to help me drink them."

"Lucky me," she teased.

A smile creased his lips. "Make that luckier me."

She rolled her eyes playfully at his remark, trying to ignore how his words made her tummy flutter. They stared at each other for a moment, and as they did, Scarlett's awareness of him flooded back.

Remembrance of Lazy Jake's. The parking lot, the fireworks, the heat. How he'd taken her mouth with his—warm, tender, sensual. Her nipples tightened, and a small sigh slipped from her lips. She briefly closed her eyes, but when she opened them again, she saw Dante had stepped away. Feeling heat rise to her face and trying to cover her feelings, she joked, "What does a girl have to do to get a drink around here?"

His eyebrows lifted.

She winced immediately realizing that probably wasn't the best thing to ask him.

"All she has to do is smile." He began lining up glasses in front of her.

With a saucy tilt of her head, she said, "Let's start with the red."

A minute later, Scarlett swirled the deep garnet liquid in her glass, watching the way the light caught the ruby hues. Dante now stood across from her, broad shoulders relaxed, his expression serious as he studied the drink in his hand.

She lifted her glass, inhaling the spice and dark fruit. She took a sip and let the flavor roll across her tongue. Smooth, bold with just enough edge to demand attention. "This one has presence. It doesn't let you ignore it."

Dante's gaze flicked to her, his lips curving into a hint of a smile. "You've got a good palate."

Her breath caught, and a tingling sensation flowed through her body. She pretended to study the wine again as though the swirling crimson could steady her emotions.

"Or maybe it's just good wine," she answered.

He chuckled low and easy and reached for another bottle. He poured the following sample into a clean glass and then handed it to her. As he did, their fingers brushed. Only for a second, but it was enough to make her heartbeat quicken.

"We should probably pace ourselves. I count six more to sample."

"I don't mind taking my time."

Ordering herself to calm down, Scarlett brought the glass to her lips. The crisp white wine burst with floral notes, but she barely tasted it. Dante was watching her, and his gaze felt unnerving. This is business, she reminded herself. But the look in his eyes told her otherwise.

* * *

Dante's stomach clenched as he watched Scarlett drive away. Tonight, as they'd sampled wine and talked, he'd been careful to avoid asking her personal questions. Instead, he joked and shared stories about growing up in New York. But when he walked her to her car and she turned to say goodnight, his gaze zeroed in on her face. Her eyes seemed to sparkle in the moonlight as she held out her hand.

"Goodnight, Dante. I had a nice time."

He took her hand in his and gave it a slight squeeze. "Me too."

She smiled, and he felt a tiny pull in his stomach. Holding the car door open, she slid into the driver's seat. As she did, he caught the vanilla scent of her shampoo along with the hint of her floral perfume. All his thoughts turned to desire. Desperately, he wanted to wrap his fingers in her thick, shiny hair and pull her to him.

Instead, he forced himself to step back and say, "Drive safe."

As the taillights of her car faded in the distance, he wondered how he would survive the next few weeks. Finally, he released a long sigh, stepped inside, and closed the door.

Chapter 9

Five days later, Dante stood in the open doorway of the Eclipse Lounge, arms crossed, watching rain hammer the ground. The new patio base was now a soggy mess. Wind whipped through the parking lot, rattling the temporary fencing, and behind him, a metal sign clanged to the ground.

He stepped outside and let his gaze roam over the patio area while ignoring the raindrops soaking through his T-shirt. The construction area looked like a flood zone. Puddles deep enough to swallow a boot, wooden forms half-submerged, a few leaned at awkward angles like they'd given up.

The rain came minutes after the contractor finished setting the forms, adding to the square footage. They had the gravel base down. The rebar was in, and the concrete pour was scheduled for the next day. But if this unexpected rain continued, they'd have to reschedule.

Talk about bad luck.

He turned to go back inside when Scarlett's car pulled into the parking lot, tires splashing through the water. He watched as she parked and, clutching her handbag to her chest, made a mad dash toward the back door he held open.

She slipped past him. "Woo, what a downpour! Was this in the forecast?"

He shook his head. "Nope."

"Hopefully, this storm clears up soon." She shrugged off her wet hoodie.

"Here, let me take that for you."

"Thanks." She handed him her hooded jacket and followed close behind as he headed to the office.

"Have a seat," he motioned toward the chair opposite his desk, then hung her jacket on a hook near the side wall. His office was just a small room off the kitchen. It consisted of a desk, two chairs, and a row of metal cabinets. But it was good enough for him. It gave him privacy when he needed it.

He slipped into his chair and glanced over at her. Several strands of her wet hair were plastered to her cheeks, and her face seemed flushed.

She met his stare and shrugged. "I know you're worried that we might lose a day, but Arizona rain starts and stops. It's normal."

"Do I look worried?"

"Well, I assume you are."

"Scarlett, have you seen the mess out there?"

"Yes, looks bad...," her voice trailed away.

Dante leaned back and let out a sigh. What was the use of yelling at her? He knew she was as upset as he was about this setback. But unlike her, he didn't see it as minor. He got up and headed for the submerged patio.

Scarlett followed him, her boots squelching through the water. "Look, it's only sprinkling now. I'll bet the sun will be shining any minute."

He ran a hand through his hair, his jaw clenched tight. "I knew this was too good to be true," he snapped. "Should've kept things simple. Should've just—"

"Dante, stop." Her voice cut him off. "We don't have time for a meltdown. We need options."

He shot her a stern look. "You think I don't know that? I know how much we lose if that patio stays a construction zone, do you?"

She stepped forward, her expression intense. "I'm not giving up. We've worked too hard." She touched his arm. "It's typical Arizona weather. Wet one minute, dry the next. Seriously, Dante, it'll be okay."

Dante's stomach twisted. Mentally, his brain shouted, it's not just about the patio— it's proving to everyone, including Dad, I can make this place work. He looked toward the East, trying not to show his anguish.

She tugged on his arm. "We have a television station coming tomorrow morning."

He nodded. But as he turned to close the back door, a white city vehicle pulled into the parking lot. It stopped, and soon a man in an orange vest and a clipboard climbed out.

Dante kept the door open.

"Good morning," the man said as he stepped inside. The pointing to his badge added, "I'm City Code Enforcement. We had an anonymous complaint regarding unpermitted structural work."

"It's just a small addition to the patio. And a cover."

The man didn't smile. "Even additions need the proper documentation. There is no permit on file, and no inspection request has been made. If concrete was poured, that's a violation."

Dante's voice rose. "It wasn't. The rain stopped it."

Scarlett stepped between them. "This is all a misunderstanding. The permits are ordered. But we're short on time. You see, we've planned a grand opening."

"I'm sorry. But until I see approved plans and the correct permits, all work halts." The inspector pulled a red sticker from his clipboard and then walked outside.

Dante followed him and watched him slap it onto the temporary fencing.

CODE VIOLATION.

"You've got to be kidding me."

"Call the Building Department," the inspector said as he walked back to his truck. "You're going to need to file a retroactive permit. It's a process."

The truck drove off, leaving the two of them staring at the red tag.

He let out a long breath. "This is bad."

"Do you want to call your dad?"

"No!" He lowered his voice. "Not yet." He turned and headed back inside.

* * *

Scarlett stood on the muddy patio, the red CODE VIOLATION notice glaring at her like a personal insult. The storm had already delayed construction, and now this. She drew a steady breath, the pressure of opening night settling like a weight on her shoulders. Pulling out her phone, she might know someone who actually knew what to do. Rebecca answered on the second ring.

"Hey, Scarlett. How's it going?"

"Not great," Scarlett admitted. "We've hit a snag with the patio. Permits and inspections. It's a mess." She hesitated, hating to ask. "Do you think your dad might have some advice?"

"He might," Rebecca said immediately. "I'll have him give you a call."

"Thank you. You're a lifesaver."

"Always," Rebecca replied. "Good luck."

Scarlett ended the call and glanced back at the glaring red notice. There was nothing to do now but wait and cross her fingers that Mr. Prentice could help.

She'd just settled on a barstool when her phone rang. She answered, and a familiar voice came on the line.

"Scarlett, it's been a while. Rebecca tells me you're having issues?"

"Yes, Sir. The city halted our patio construction due to a permit issue. We're so close to having a grand opening. This could derail everything." She forced her tone steady, aware of how desperate she sounded, then quickly added, "I don't expect you to go out of your way, just hoping you might have some advice."

"Since retirement, I don't have the clout I once did, but I'll offer some guidance. Call the city's Small Business Assistance office. They're there to help with situations like yours. Meanwhile, I'll try to get the name of someone who can expedite the process."

"Thank you so much."

"I'm happy to help you, Scarlett."

As the call ended, a renewed sense of hope washed over her. With Rebecca's dad's guidance and connections, there had to be a way to move this project forward.

Chapter 10

Dante stood at the bar, jaw clenched as he stared at the construction schedule.

"He told me that we should start with the city's Small Business Assistance office," Scarlett said, stepping beside him. "Sometimes they can reduce the amount of red tape for new businesses on tight deadlines." She gave him a victorious look.

He laughed. "Who said?"

"My friend."

"You think they'll fast-track our permit because you know a guy?"

"Well, I didn't say that." She huffed a breath. "Look, Dante, I'm trying to help. Senator Prentice might know someone at City Planning."

"You went to a senator?"

"He's a retired senator," she said calmly. "He's my friend Rebecca's dad. I didn't think it would hurt to ask."

A long pause stretched between them.

"I just don't want to owe anyone. Not your friend's dad. Not mine."

She stepped closer and rested her hand on his arm. "This isn't about owing. It's about surviving. You wanted that patio done, right?"

He nodded once, almost reluctant. "Yeah. I still do."

"Good. Then let me make the calls and push the paperwork. You keep the rest of this place moving."

Another beat passed. The fight drained out of his eyes, and he scrubbed a hand over his face. "All right. But if some city planner shows up tomorrow asking who we bribed, I hope you have an answer."

She cracked a smile. "We'll offer them a VIP table and the best tequila on hand."

That drew the smallest curve of a grin from him. "You're serious about having this place up and ready by the opening, huh?"

Her smile remained, and she lifted her chin. "You bet I am. I've already sent out invitations to the local VIP's. People have us on their calendars. Cancelling or delaying could ruin us." She took a breath. "Dante, I believe in you and your vision.

* * *

Dante studied Scarlett for a long moment, longer than he should have. Her eyes gleamed with certainty, her whole posture radiating the kind of fight he both admired and feared. She wasn't just invested in this project—she was invested in *him*. And that rattled him more than any delay from City Planning.

The truth of that sank under his skin. His fingers tightened around the clipboard, then he set it down again with a sigh. "Do what you have to do. But don't expect me to sit around waiting for politicians to solve my problems. I've got a kitchen to run and a staff to train."

"Good," she said softly, as if his stubbornness was precisely what she'd counted on.

Dante turned, needing space, needing distance, but his eyes caught on her again. The tilt of her chin. The spark in her eyes. She had a way of drawing him in, even when his instincts screamed to keep her at arm's length.

He dragged in a breath, forcing his focus back to the task list. "If we're going to make this work, we can't afford one more misstep."

"Then we won't have one," she replied, steady as a promise.

Something in his chest shifted at the unfamiliar sense of trust he hadn't asked for but couldn't reasonably refuse. He didn't know if it was her determination or her faith in *him*, but for the first time since this whole mess started, he believed they might pull it off.

Chapter 11

Scarlett entered the parking lot of Eclipse Lounge just as her phone rang. When she saw who it was, she quickly pulled into an empty slot, threw the car in park, and answered. "Hello?"

"Scarlett? This is Wendy from the Planning and Zoning Department. I'm calling about the issue with your property."

She forced herself to stay calm. "Please tell me you have good news."

A pause. Never a good sign.

"Unfortunately, well...it's complicated."

"How complicated?" Her stomach knotted, and she pressed her lips together.

"The patio addition extends into a buffer zone that wasn't accounted for in the original plans. The city is requiring a full review."

Scarlett closed her eyes. "You're kidding."

"A review process can take up to six or eight weeks, sometimes longer. I'm trying to push for an emergency variance hearing, but no promises."

"So, we might not be able to finish the patio at all?"

"I'm saying…it's just not a quick fix. But I'm working on it."

Scarlett thanked her, ended the call, and sat in silence, her fingers tightening around the steering wheel. The patio had been her signature touch; the thing she thought would make the night special. The scheduled opening night was getting closer every day, and now the one thing she'd been most excited about was buried in red tape.

She entered the lounge and found Dante behind the bar, counting bottles and muttering under his breath.

"How's it going?" he asked when she approached.

She dropped her bag onto the bar top. "Bad. Zoning issue. We're in a protected buffer zone—something the city missed."

His head snapped up. "You're kidding."

She shrugged. "They're doing a review, but it could take weeks, even months."

The look he shot her was clearly not happy. "I knew this was a bad idea from the start."

"So now you're blaming me?"

"I'm not blaming anyone," he said, voice clipped. "I'm just worried about what happens if that patio stays a construction zone."

She drew a steadying breath, "Look, I get your concern, Dante. But I can't give up."

He met her gaze. After a beat, he sighed and splayed both his hands on the counter. "That's it, Scarlett. We open without the patio. I'll squeeze in a few more tables inside."

"No. We need the extra room."

He arched a brow. "Got a miracle up your sleeve?"

"Maybe." A slow smile formed. "We fake it."

He blinked. "Fake it?"

"Yeah. Make it look finished. Rent some big planters, string lights, maybe artificial turf. It'll be smaller than we wanted, but it will be nice and add some additional space."

He studied her for a moment, then ran a hand through his hair. "We've got the health department's approval for the area as is from when we originally applied. So, if the liquor license extension comes soon, we're good. It just won't be as large an area as we hoped."

"Yes." Her grin broke wide. "We can do this." Before she knew it, she'd thrown her arms around his neck—and kissed him.

She jerked back. "Oh, God...I'm sorry." Her hand flew to her mouth.

His lips curved, slow and teasing. "Wow. I should agree with you more often."

Heat flooded her cheeks. "I, uh, have work to do." She spun before he could say a word, her pulse hammering.

"Sure," he said. "I'll be right here, agreeing with you."

Dante froze. One second, she'd been grinning at him, eyes bright, the next, her lips were on his. The kiss was brief, but it hit him like a live wire. For a split second, every rational thought disappeared.

If this were any other situation, he'd have kissed her back without hesitation. But this wasn't just anyone. This was Scarlett. His event planner. The woman helping him keep alive the dream he'd worked for his whole life.

He stayed rooted to the floor, pulse hammering, while his brain shouted *don't*

He'd learned the hard way that mixing work with desire burned more than bridges. It burned futures. And right now, he couldn't afford that. Not with Eclipse Lounge, his shot to prove to his father that he could stand on his own. And yet... Scarlett made that focus impossible.

She wasn't just beautiful. She was relentless, clever, completely unshakable. He admired her drive. Admiration was safe. But the pull under it—the way her voice tightened when she argued, the faint scent of citrus and vanilla when she walked by him, were the things that kept him awake at night.

He exhaled, trying to shake it off. "I'll be in the kitchen if you need me." He turned before he could do something stupid. Like reach for her again.

Chapter 12

The Eclipse Lounge's grand opening night had arrived. And Scarlett was ready. On paper, at least. She'd spent every waking hour buried in final details, determined to prove she could make this night fabulous.

So far, her morning had started like any other, if any other included half the staff running on caffeine and mild panic. She stood in the middle of the restaurant, headset on, clipboard clutched, and coffee in hand. Her voice was calm. Her pulse, not so much.

"Okay, team," she called out. "We open in six hours. That's three hundred and sixty minutes, or—if you prefer panic math—twenty-one thousand, six hundred seconds."

Someone laughed. Someone else groaned. Scarlett took it as progress. She ticked items off her list as she paced between tables.

"Linens? Perfect. Silverware? Counted. Sound check?" She turned toward the small dance floor and stage. "Where's our sound guy?"

Dante emerged from the kitchen, sleeves rolled up, looking infuriatingly composed for a man juggling ten thousand details. "Probably tuning the speakers or meditating. I'm told both are important for acoustics."

She shot him a stern look over her clipboard.

With a laugh, he said, "You're impressive when you boss people around."

"I'm not bossing. I'm delegating."

"Right. And the difference is...?"

"The paycheck."

He laughed, a low rumble that somehow steadied her heartbeat. "You keep this up, and I'll owe you hazard pay."

"Already filled out the form," she teased. "Under emotional labor."

A crash came from the back hall.

She winced. "Tell me that wasn't a tray of our dishes."

Dante muttered and headed toward the noise.

By the time he returned, Scarlett had moved to the bar, rearranging drink menus.

"Well?" she asked.

"Good news and bad," he said, wiping his hands. "Bad news: we're down one bus tub of dishes and the dishwasher's ego. Good news: the floor is sparkling."

"Excellent," she said dryly. "I'll add it to the cleaning report."

Just then, her headset crackled. "Scarlett? Uh, we have a situation."

She pressed the mic. "What kind of situation, Tina?"

"The flowers. They're... um... wrong."

Scarlett closed her eyes. "Define wrong."

"They're daisies. Yellow. Lots of them. You ordered orchids."

Dante raised a brow. "Big difference?"

She turned to him. "How do you feel about owning the most cheerful steakhouse in Arizona?"

"Not great," he said. "I was going for sultry, not sunshine."

Scarlett sighed and grabbed her bag. "I'll fix it."

He moved in front of her. "You've been here since dawn. I'll go."

"Do you know the difference between orchids and daisies?"

"I can learn."

"Not in time."

A grin tugged at one corner of his mouth. "You have control issues."

"You have a hero complex."

"Fine," he said, holding up his hands. "But if you pass out from exhaustion tonight, the blame's on you."

"Noted." She moved past him, trying to ignore the fact that her arm brushed his on the way out. And that her pulse leaped like it had been waiting for that exact collision. She turned back. "I need Joe and his truck."

* * *

Two hours later, Dante could finally breathe again. Scarlett had returned with a car full of white orchids and a completely different attitude, still bossy, but softer around the edges. From where he stood near the kitchen, he watched her move through the main room. Focused, precise, all business. But every so often, a small smile flickered across her face as all the chaos came together. The sight of her smile sent an electric rush of energy through him, just like the first time he'd seen her at Lazy Jake's.

Walking to the prep counter, he grabbed a small plate. When he found her, she was standing at a table, making a note on her list of paperwork. "Try this," he said.

She turned and pushed a strand of hair behind her ear. "What is it?"

"My signature *amuse-bouche* for our guests." He held out a small white spoon.

The spoon held a delicate swirl of pale mousse, topped with a single basil leaf and a shimmer of lemon oil. She tasted it. Cool, airy, and bright, the citrus melting into something creamy and unexpected.

"Lime and basil?" she guessed.

"Close. Lemon and mint," he said, watching her. "It's supposed to be refreshing."

"It's perfect."

And before he could stop himself, he said quietly, gazing into her eyes, "Yeah. It is."

For one suspended heartbeat, the atmosphere changed. It was just her, with that spark in her eyes, and him, standing there, feeling like a devoted puppy.

Then the door swung open.

"Delivery!" A guy rolled in a cart stacked high with champagne crates. "Sorry, traffic on the 101. Where do you want these?"

Instantly in professional mode, Scarlett said, "Bar storage, please. Carefully."

Dante cleared his throat, moving aside. He watched her go, the sway of her walk at odds with the crisp, no-nonsense tone she used with the staff. That spark she carried had no business getting under his skin.

He turned back to the bar, pretending to study the champagne labels.

Focus, Rivera.

Food, guests, and his father. He had enough to juggle without adding her to the list. But as her laughter floated across the room, light and unguarded, he knew he was already in trouble. She was a woman who could do what no other had ever done, break his heart.

Chapter 13

Here we go, Scarlett thought as she stood near the Eclipse Lounge's entrance. She smoothed her hands down her black cocktail dress and took a slow breath. The room looked incredible. Golden light shimmered off glassware, creating a distinct ambiance of elegance. Soft music spilled from the speakers, and the hum of conversation promised the night would be a success.

Every server, dressed in black slacks and white shirts, weaved between tables with practiced smiles, keeping complimentary champagne flutes filled. Even the fake patio, her desperate, last-minute fix, glowed under its canopy of string lights as if it had always been the design. And the evening weather was a beautiful sixty-seven degrees.

Across the room, Dante stood behind the bar, in a black suit, tie loosened, wearing that smile that always turned her knees to jelly. She didn't look away, just took a moment to absorb the sight of him. He looked good enough to make her forget the checklist clutched in her hand.

He caught her eye and offered a slight nod, all business. She returned it, equally composed.

Perfect. Professional. Totally fine.

Her pulse disagreed.

He crossed the room to join her. "You ready?" he asked.

"I've been ready since five a.m.," she said. "Well, mostly."

"By the way, you look gorgeous."

"Thanks." She reached out and brushed a speck of dust from his sleeve. "Not bad yourself."

"Yeah?" His eyebrows lifted, and he gave a soft chuckle. "Well, thank you."

His quiet laugh sent a ripple of warmth sliding through her.

"Seriously, Scarlett, you've done an incredible job. I had my doubts about your paint choice for the accent wall, but under this lighting, it's perfect."

"You doubted me?" she teased.

"Maybe a little." His grin deepened before he checked his watch. "It's about time to serve the first course. I'm going to make sure the patio's running smoothly, then head to the kitchen. Come with me?"

She nodded, and he stepped back, letting her move ahead of him. As she passed, his hand brushed the small of her back. The contact was brief, but it sent a shiver through her anyway.

"The patio is perfect," she added lightly. "The florist worked magic with the planters.

Guests seem to love it. All my friends included."

"Glad to hear. By the way, I'd like to meet these friends of yours," he said. His tone had changed. It seemed personal rather than professional.

"They're excited to meet you."

As soon as they stepped outside, it was as if they'd entered a garden. Planters overflowing with greenery and flowers hid any imperfections, while strands of golden lights cast a soft, romantic glow over the tables. Laughter floated through the air, glasses clinked, and conversation wove together with the faint whisper of a cool evening breeze.

Exactly how she'd envisioned, smaller, of course, and missing the firepit and water feature, but they could be added once the construction permits were approved. For now, it was perfect. Welcoming, elegant, and a little magical.

Scarlett spotted her friends at a corner table. A very pregnant Rebecca waved the moment she saw her, and her husband, Mick, rose politely to greet them. Beside them, Trisha, still wearing that newlywed glow, had her hand looped through Colton's arm, while Rayna, single and unbothered, laughed at something one of the servers said.

"Everyone," Scarlett said as she reached the table, "I'd like you to meet Dante Riveria, the manager and chef in charge of the amazing food you're about to enjoy. Dante, these are my friends—Rebecca and Mick, Trisha and Colton, and, of course, you already know Rayna.”

Dante offered a warm nod to the women, then shook hands with the men. “Thank you for coming tonight. It means a lot to me, and I know it does to Scarlett, too.”

The way he included her caught her off guard. When he’d said her name, aligning their success, it settled deep, tugging at the wall she’d tried to keep between them.

Rebecca’s look was all too readable: *he’s even better in person.* Rayna’s raised brows added her own unspoken commentary. Scarlett ignored both, quickly redirecting the conversation to the menu and the patio design.

Still, as laughter and chatter swirled around them, a quiet ache pressed at her chest. The night was everything she’d hoped for, a triumph. And yet, she also knew that when the lights dimmed and the last of the guests left, her job was done.

So was her time with Dante.

And that, she realized, was the part she wasn’t ready to let go of yet.

* * *

Dante looked around and couldn’t help but smile. Scarlett had crushed it. The guest list read like a who’s who of the Valley.

Politicians, TV personalities, reporters, and business leaders. The energy buzzed, and the food was leaving the kitchen perfectly plated. He couldn't have asked for a better night.

And yet, beneath the surface, unease churned. This wasn't just about a smooth grand opening. It was about proving something to himself, and to the man who still saw him as careless, impulsive, and untested.

He left Scarlett chatting with her friends and moved to another table, thanking the guests and soaking in their compliments. For the first time all evening, he actually let himself breathe.

Then someone tapped his shoulder. He turned and immediately knew something was wrong.

Joe stood there, pale and tense, cell phone clutched in his hand. "I'm sorry," he said, voice tight. "I've got to go. My wife's in the ER. It's bad."

The words hit hard. Dante's first instinct was to push back. Tell him he couldn't just walk out now, not tonight, but one look at Joe's face killed the thought.

"Go," he said, clapping his shoulder. "Don't waste time. I'll take over."

Joe was gone a moment later, slipping out the back. Dante's stomach knotted. Without a bartender, the entire rhythm of the night would collapse. Drinks fueled the crowd, kept the energy alive, and right now, the bar was packed.

He scanned the room and spotted Scarlett, still at the table with her friends. He hated to interrupt, but there was no choice. It only took him a moment to reach her side. Leaning close, he whispered into her ear. "We've got a problem."

Her smile vanished. "What happened?"

"Bartender's gone. Family emergency. The bar's about to explode, I'm going to take over." He turned to leave. But before he took a step, she grabbed his arm.

"Wait. I have an idea." Still holding his arm, she turned to her friends. "Rayna, we need your bartending skills."

Rayna blinked. "Excuse me?"

"It's an emergency," Scarlett said. "Our bartender left. Could you please help us?"

Rayna looked startled, then skeptical. "You want *me*?"

Dante studied her. Rayna was the friend of Scarlett's that he'd met at Lazy Jake's. Purple in her hair, and a face that said I'd rather be drinking the cocktails, not making them. *Was she really capable?*

Then Mick chimed in. "She's the best bartender I have. You have to promise, it's only for tonight."

Without hesitation, Dante said, "Done." He offered Rayna a grateful smile. "I'd appreciate the help more than you know."

She grinned. "Guess I'm hired."

Relief surged through him so fast he almost laughed. "I'll owe you big time."

Rayna was already standing. "Relax. I've got this."

Laughter rippled around the table, the tension breaking like a snapped string. Dante exhaled, but his gaze stayed on Scarlett. She was calm, composed, already scanning the patio like she was back in command. And for the first time all night, he realized the truth. She wasn't just holding the evening together. She was holding *him* together, too.

Rayna moved toward the bar, slipping easily into motion as if she'd been part of the staff all along. Within minutes, the clatter of shakers and the hum of conversation blended again, the near-crisis already smoothing itself out.

Dante took a moment to breathe. The chaos was under control, but his pulse wasn't. Across the patio, Scarlett was giving quiet directions to a server. The overhead light haloed her hair, catching in the loose waves that brushed her shoulders. She looked absolutely stunning.

When she finally glanced toward him, a spark of shared relief flickered between them, and something he couldn't quite name.

He crossed to her. "You just saved my night again."

She gave a short laugh. "That's twice now. I think I will start charging extra."

"Worth every penny," he murmured before he could stop himself.

She tilted her head, a teasing glint in her eyes. "Careful, Rivera. Someone might think you're flirting with your event planner."

"Someone might be right," he said softly, almost to himself.

The words lingered between them before she looked away, pretending to check on a nearby table. After a moment, she turned back to him, "Let's make sure your new bartender has everything she needs."

Dante nodded. But as they walked side by side, a sudden thought pressed hard in his chest. After tonight, she'd no longer be employed by his company. All the reasons she kept him at arm's length would be removed.

Chapter 14

Scarlett smiled to herself as she wove through the kitchen, sidestepping cooks who were busy cleaning up for the night. If the Eclipse Lounge had nights like this every weekend, Dante would have no problem making it a success.

At the office door, she tapped lightly before easing it open and peeking inside. Dante sat hunched at his desk, the glow of the computer screen carving sharp light across his face. His jaw was tight and focused until she spoke.

"Hi," she said softly.

His head lifted, and the tension in his expression softened.

"So," she asked, "was the night a success?"

"Better than I'd hoped." He leaned forward, resting one elbow on the desk. "Thanks to you." His voice dropped. "Seriously, Scarlett. You're the one who made this happen."

He gestured for her to sit.

"Thank you. But you had a lot to do with it. It was your menu, after all."

"And a great team of chefs." He chuckled. "Plus, your friend Rayna. She doubled the drink sales I expected for tonight."

Scarlett smiled. "She's amazing."

"Yeah," he murmured. "So are you."

Silence stretched between them. The muffled clatter of pans drifted in from the kitchen, along with the scent of roasted garlic and lemon butter. The rest of the world blurred until there were only the two of them in the soft glow of the office light.

Her breath caught. She needed to say something to break the spell, but no words came.

Dante stood and stepped closer, until she had to tilt her chin to meet his gaze. "You have no idea how much I needed someone like you tonight," he said quietly.

Her pulse stumbled. She reminded herself to stay professional, but when his fingers brushed her arm, his thumb tracing a feather-light line along her skin, every logical thought scattered.

He offered his hand. Hesitant, she took it, and he pulled her to her feet. The space between them dissolved, her breath mingling with his. All she had to do was close her eyes—

A sharp knock at the door splintered the moment.

"Hey, Dante, are you busy?" Rayna called.

Scarlett jerked back, heat flooding her cheeks.

Dante muttered something under his breath and straightened, although his hand lingered a second too long before he let her go.

Rayna slipped in, her eyes flicking between the two of them. One brow arched. "Ohhh. Sorry, I didn't mean to interrupt."

Scarlett shot her a look that could curdle milk, but Rayna seemed to ignore the meaning. She grinned. "Dante, someone wants to see you."

"Thank you. I'll be right out," he said.

"I need to go check the guests," Scarlett said briskly as she ushered Rayna out of the office.

Rayna fell into step beside her, smirking. "Well... should I ask how close I came to catching Dante making a move on my bestie, or just assume?"

Scarlett nearly tripped. "Rayna—"

"Don't even try," Rayna said, cutting her off. "That was not a business-meeting face you were making in there."

"We were just talking."

"Mmhmm. Talking. With your eyes closed?"

Scarlett groaned while glancing around, making sure no one was in earshot. "Stop. Someone might hear you."

Rayna grinned, clearly enjoying every second. "There's no one around."

"Still, you never know, and I don't need any gossip getting back to my company."

Rayna lowered her voice. "I'm just saying... grand opening, sparks flying, and my best friend front and center. Looks like this place isn't the only thing with a promising future."

Scarlett blew out a breath and gave her a flat look, though she couldn't quite smother her smile. "You are insufferable."

"And you are blushing."

Scarlett exhaled, but beneath Rayna's teasing, she couldn't shake the memory of Dante's eyes, his voice, the way he'd leaned in like—

Forcing the thought away, she told her friend, "I'm exhausted. She made her way to the bar and eased onto a stool.

Rayna followed and stepped behind the bar. "I've never seen a man look at you like that. Trust me, I notice these things. It's literally my job."

"You're making this into something it's not."

"Uh-huh. So, you didn't *want* him to kiss you?"

She didn't speak, then realized silence was an answer.

Rayna grinned, triumphant. "Thought so."

Scarlett groaned again, burying her face in her folded arms on the bar. "You're relentless."

"Of course, I am. This is the most exciting thing to happen to you in... well, a long time. Here, have some champagne." She filled a glass from an open bottle.

"Thanks." She took a sip, hoping the bubbles would calm her nerves.

"Uh-oh," Rayna murmured, glancing toward the kitchen. "Speak of the devil."

Scarlett turned, and her heart gave an unhelpful leap. Dante was walking toward them, sleeves rolled, a satisfied smile on his face.

He came to the bar and handed Rayna an envelope. "Pay for tonight. And thank you again."

"You don't owe me anything. This is what friends do. Besides, I made great tips."

"Nope. You get paid."

"You're a good guy, Rivera."

He chuckled. "That's debatable." He glanced at Scarlett, winked, then turned back to Rayna. "Someone wants to see me?"

Rayna gestured to a man near the wall, studying a painting of the desert.

Dante nodded and walked off.

"Almost everyone is gone, so I'm going to head out. Unless you need me to hang around?" Rayna said as she grabbed her purse and dropped the envelope inside.

"Don't be silly. Go home."

"I'll call you tomorrow. We have a baby shower to host."

"And by the looks of her, we'd better do it soon."

"Right," Rayna answered as she headed for the front door.

Scarlett straightened on her stool and picked up her drink, then swiveled around enough to see Dante talking to a well-dressed man. The two laughed, and after a moment, they shook hands. When the man left, Dante locked up, the last guest gone for the night. She knew any servers still inside would use the back exit. Curiosity built as he strode toward her, wearing a huge smile.

"What a night," he said, sliding onto the stool beside her. "You'll never guess who that was."

"I'll bite. Who?"

"A food critic. Wants to feature the restaurant on his blog." He stepped behind the bar, grabbed a beer, and twisted the top. "Said the food blew him away."

"That's incredible,"

"Yeah," he replied, taking a drink. He set the bottle down, eyes glinting. "You know what else is incredible? The music."

She listened. Frank Sinatra's smooth voice crooned from the speakers.

"When Old Blue Eyes sings," he said, offering his hand, "you *have* to dance."

She laughed. "You *have* to dance?"

"Pretty sure it's a rule."

"Well, I'd hate to break a rule."

She took his hand, and he pulled her close.

* * *

Scarlett's head rested lightly against his shoulder as they swayed to the romantic music drifting from the overhead speakers. The familiar scent of vanilla curled around him, sweet and familiar, along with something else he couldn't put his finger on. But whatever the fragrance was, it had his pulse racing.

He tightened his hold, guiding her in slow steps that matched the lazy rhythm of Sinatra's voice. She fit against him perfectly, like they'd done this a hundred times instead of now twice. The first time at Lazy Jake's and tonight on a whim.

"This is nice," he murmured, his hand gliding to the small of her back.

She hummed in agreement, the sound low and content.

He could stay like this forever. The room was quiet, her body warm against his, their movements effortless and unhurried.

The song began to wind down, finally coming to an end. He didn't want to let her go. When she lifted her head, her eyes caught his, soft and searching. The rest of the room seemed to fade; for that moment, it was just the two of them. He brushed his thumb along her cheek, the lightest touch, and leaned in close enough to feel her breath. Her lips parted just slightly. Whether in invitation or warning, he couldn't tell.

"Dante..." she whispered. Her voice trembled slightly. "Thank you for the dance." She pulled back slightly.

"You're welcome," he murmured, his voice huskier than he intended. He didn't step away.

"I should probably go home." Her smile was teasing now, the kind that made him forget logic entirely. The tip of her tongue darted out to wet her lips, and he almost groaned.

"Yeah. You've had a long day."

"I really hope you do well here."

"Are you worried about me?"

"No. The restaurant is beautiful and you're a wonderful chef."

"Thank you. That means a lot coming from you." His gaze held hers, then he gave her a slow grin. "Are you hungry?"

She tilted her head, a spark of curiosity in her eyes. "That depends. What are you offering?"

"There's a tray of desserts left in the kitchen. Interested?"

Her smile widened, playful and slow. "You had me at dessert."

Chapter 15

Everyone had left, the front lights were dimmed, and the doors were all locked. She and Dante were entirely alone in the kitchen. Scarlett leaned against the workstation counter and watched as he pulled a tray of desserts from the refrigerator. "Anything I can do?" she asked.

"There's an open bottle of champagne at the bar. Unless you'd rather have coffee, I can make some."

Her brows lifted. "Champagne sounds perfect. After all, we are celebrating."

He gave her a slow smile that sent flutters through her tummy.

He held her gaze for a long moment before pointing toward the tray. "What's your preference? There's cheesecake, chocolate lava cake, and it looks like some crème brûlée. Anything look good to you?"

"Chocolate works for me." Her voice had slightly shaken, and she hoped he hadn't noticed. No man made her this nervous, and it was really beginning to tick her off.

"Perfect choice. I'll warm it up."

"I'll get the champagne." She headed to the bar, grabbed two glasses, and the bottle.

By the time she returned, he was pouring warmed-up chocolate sauce over a large piece of dark fudge cake. The air smelled of rich, mouth-watering chocolate.

"Looks delicious," she said as she filled each glass with the sparkling beverage.

He looked up and grinned. "Yes. The cake looks good, too."

Flutters skittered in her tummy again. She giggled as she pushed a glass toward him.

"To friendships," he said as they clinked their glasses together in a toast.

They each took a drink before she lowered her glass and said, "I'm glad you asked me to stay."

"I couldn't let you go without offering you dessert." His voice sounded sincere. He held her gaze for a long moment before asking, "Whipped cream?"

She swallowed hard. "Sure."

She sipped her champagne and watched as Dante spooned a generous dollop of whipped cream on the top of the cake. He slid the plate between them and scooped up a generous forkful. Holding the fork toward her, he said, "Try it."

She hesitated for a second, then leaned in and opened her mouth. Her eyes closed, and she slowly chewed, savoring the decadent sweetness.

"Oh, I'm definitely taking this." She reached for the plate.

"You're not even going to pretend to share?"

"Not a chance." She grinned, snagging a fork. "You had your moment of glory tonight. I'm claiming this one."

He laughed, the sound easy and low. "All right, I'll allow it. But only because you saved my life about six times today."

"Six? I thought it was at least seven."

She took another bite, letting her eyes close for just a second. "Oh, wow. This is ridiculous."

"Good?" he asked.

She pointed the fork at him. "You might have created the perfect dessert."

He leaned against the workstation counter, arms crossed. "You make it look better than it tastes."

Scarlett blinked. "Was that supposed to be a compliment?"

"Maybe." His grin was slow, lazy. "Depends on how you take it."

She rolled her eyes, but her smile didn't fade. "Careful, Dante. I might start thinking you're flirting with me again."

He stepped beside her, voice quieting. "Who says I ever stopped?"

Her breath hitched. She lowered the fork. "You really shouldn't say things like that."

"Why not?"

"Because I might believe you."

"Scarlett," he spoke her name quietly. "You're not under contract anymore. The event is over."

"That's right, but..." She let her words trail away.

"Do you ever think about that night we met?"

"Sometimes." Every day, but she wasn't going to say that to him.

"I dream about what might have happened if we weren't interrupted." He'd moved closer.

"You dream about me?"

"All the time." He whispered as his hand lifted, and he ran a finger slowly along the side of her neck.

A shiver ran through her. He was right, her job here was finished. But did she dare? What kind of relationship would they have? He wasn't staying in Arizona permanently. By next year, he'd return to New York. Or Paris. Still....

His hand moved higher, and he brushed her hair from her cheek. "There's nothing to stop us now."

"I don't want to be hurt."

"I won't hurt you, Scarlett. I promise."

Had he understood what she was saying? Or was he telling her what he thought she wanted to hear? The flutters in her tummy increased.

For a heartbeat, neither moved. Then she placed the fork down, still unsure what to say.

The silence stretched.

"Scarlett..." He hesitated, as if weighing his words. "I've worked for years to make nights like this happen. But I think tonight was perfect because you were here."

Her breath caught. His words didn't seem rehearsed. They sounded sincere.

She looked up at him, "Dante..."

He smiled faintly, as if reading her uncertainty. "Don't worry. I'm not asking for anything. Just wanted you to know."

Scarlett exhaled slowly, her lips curving into a soft, genuine smile. "Thank you. For tonight. For everything."

He reached out, brushing his knuckles along her arm. "Anytime."

For a heartbeat, neither moved. At that moment, she wasn't sure if she wanted to walk away or close the gap between them.

Her pulse thudded in her throat as he lifted his hand and traced his fingers along the curve of her shoulders. She tilted her head and gazed into his eyes. His fingers were still touching her shoulders as he dipped his head, their foreheads brushing first, then his lips found hers.

The kiss started slow, hesitant, but deepened with every second. His hand slid to the small of her back, drawing her closer until she melted against him. Then, in one motion, he grabbed her waist and lifted her onto the workstation's counter, his hips between her spread knees.

His hands were still on her waist when he broke the kiss. "You realize this changes everything."

"I'm counting on it."

He chuckled. "Good. Because I'll stop right now if that's what you want. But I know I sure don't want to."

"Then don't."

Scarlett kissed Dante hard, with all her pent-up passion. He moaned against her mouth, deepening the kiss, his hands tangled in her hair. Within that moment, she forgot everything: the work relationship, forbidden love, and that they were in the kitchen of his restaurant. All that mattered was that they were together.

* * *

His hands moved to her breasts and cupped them through the material of her dress. Then he moved his fingers upward and carefully slid the narrow straps from her shoulders, letting the fabric fall just enough to reveal more of her creamy skin. He paused, breath catching, then, with a slight tug, the material slid to her waist. He audibly gasped at how beautiful she looked to him.

Her nipples tightened beneath his gaze, and he couldn't wait any longer to touch them. He began to tease them with his fingertips as he kissed her again. She sighed

126

as their mouths moved together, kissing hard and roughly with their passion. Crushed her to him and buried his face between her ample cleavage, his body responding to her allure.

"Scarlett," he whispered against her skin. "I'm glad you don't wear a bra."

She moaned and dug her hands into his hair. "Comes in handy," she whispered.

"Yeah." With one hand, he reached beside him and grabbed the bowl of whipped cream, then smoothed it around each rosy nipple, as if he were decorating a cake. Setting the bowl aside, he looked at her and nearly came undone.

She was leaning back slightly, gazing at him through half-closed eyes. Her thick hair flowed over her shoulders in waves, and her nipples were covered entirely in delicious swirls of whipped cream. His mouth watered at the sight.

He'd been with many women in his lifetime, but never one who made him feel like this. It was wonderful and scary at the same time. With a sigh, he bent forward and ran his tongue across one nipple, savoring the sweet taste. She moaned, and her body arched, giving him better access.

Dessert finished, he whispered near her ear, "I want to make love to you."

"I want you too," she whispered back. She reached for his shirt and jerked it from his dress pants. Dante sucked in a sharp breath as her fingers slid underneath the crisp material to touch his bare skin. They moved lower to the waistband of his pants, but he stopped her.

"I don't have protection." He hadn't planned this, hadn't expected it.

She didn't answer, only stared at him as if trying to process what he was telling her.

"Come home with me. There are things that I want to do with you that require a big bed, candlelight, maybe a bathtub."

"I'd like that."

"Do you mind waiting?"

Her eyes appeared slightly glazed, but she offered him a smile. "Not if you promise it will be worth it."

"I'll definitely make that promise." He helped her adjust her dress, but not before kissing each nipple once more.

Chapter 16

The scent of coffee and something buttery drifted through the bedroom, tugging Scarlett from a deep sleep. For a moment, she didn't move. She just smiled, remembering the way Dante's hands had felt, touching every part of her. She'd never had a man make her feel the way he did.

He'd made love to her all night. Slow and easy at first, raining kisses along her throat, down to her shoulder, taking his time with her breasts, moving lower until she was almost crazy from wanting him.

Then it changed. Harder, faster, wonderful. She'd arched to him, wanting to beg him never to stop. But all that escaped her throat were more moans of pleasure. The first time he'd made her come was explosive. He'd whispered near her ear how he couldn't stop thinking about her, and that was all it took. She'd ground herself against him, calling his name as her climax rocked through her.

She sighed at the memory.

The aroma of coffee and food drifted in again. Suddenly famished, she rolled out of bed and found one of his T-shirts draped over a chair and slipped it over her head. It hung loose on her, reaching mid-thigh, soft from too many washings, and smelling faintly of spice. She padded barefoot down the hall, following the clatter of dishes and the loud Metallica tune.

The kitchen was a gleaming expanse of stainless steel and sunlight, and in the middle of it stood Dante, barefoot, jeans slung low, flipping an omelet like he owned the place. Which, technically, because it was a rental house, he didn't.

He glanced over his shoulder, a grin tugging at his mouth. "Morning, Sleeping Beauty."

"Morning," she said, voice still rough from sleep. "Are you... cooking?"

"Can't fool you." He laughed. "I'm a chef. What else would I be doing?"

"I don't know," she said, crossing the room. "Brooding? Staring moodily out the window?"

"Only on Tuesdays."

She grabbed a mug off the counter and bumped him with her hip.

He laughed again. "I make an excellent apology omelet."

"For what?"

"For being too loud and waking you. For being irresistible. Take your pick."

Scarlett rolled her eyes, but she couldn't stop smiling as she reached for the coffee pot. "You're ridiculous."

"Maybe. But you're still here."

She filled the mug. And since she preferred her first cup without cream and sugar, she took a sip. "Okay, I'll give you this—you make a mean cup of coffee."

"I grind the beans myself," he said, sounding serious. "It's an art form. The secret's in the ratio."

"Mr. Perfection." She wandered closer, eyeing the skillet. "What are you making?"

"Crab omelets with tarragon hollandaise," he said, flipping a piece of toast onto a plate. "And avocado toast for good measure. I have a reputation to uphold."

She laughed, shaking her head. "A reputation for what, showing off?"

He handed her a knife and pointed toward a cutting board. "For excellence. You, Miss Event Planner, can slice those tomatoes. Thin. Presentation matters."

"Bossy much?"

"Only in a kitchen with my sous chef."

She gave him a look that earned her a slow smile before she turned her attention to the tomatoes. "Do you cook like this every morning?"

"When I'm trying to impress someone."

"And how's that working out for you?"

He leaned an elbow on the kitchen island's counter, watching her with that same easy confidence that had undone her from the start. "Well, you're wearing my shirt, helping me make breakfast. I'd say pretty well."

She smirked and pointed the knife in his direction. "Careful, Rivera. Arrogance is not an aphrodisiac."

"Neither is a knife," he countered, catching her wrist lightly as she reached for another tomato. "Let me."

Their fingers brushed, and for a moment, the teasing quieted. The air between them hummed with tenderness as he made quick work of slicing the tomato.

She laughed watching him. "I could have done that just as nicely."

He grinned as he grabbed the skillet, slipped the finished omelet onto a plate, and slid it toward her. "Confidence. I like that."

He slid a second plate across the counter and nodded toward the stools. "Sit. Chef's orders."

Scarlett arched a brow but obeyed, pulling up the stool and tucking her bare legs beneath her.

* * *

The sunlight hit her hair just right, warm gold streaking through the dark, tousled waves. Dante had to look away before he burned the second omelet.

He joined her at the island, plates between them, and two steaming mugs of coffee. Metallica still played in the background, but he'd lowered the volume enough so they could talk.

Scarlett took her first bite and, after a minute, spoke. "Okay," she said, pointing her fork at her plate. "This might be the best breakfast I've ever had."

"I should hope so," he said, mock offense in his voice. "That hollandaise took an embarrassing amount of whisking."

She laughed. "Aw. You are trying to impress me."

He leaned his elbows on the island counter, chin propped in his hand. "My momma taught me always to be a good host."

She took another bite, swallowed, then smiled. "Thank your momma for me."

They ate in companionable silence for a few minutes, the only sounds the clink of forks and music. Every so often, their knees brushed under the counter, and she didn't pull away. He caught himself watching her more than eating.

When she glanced up, catching him staring, he didn't bother to hide it.

"What?" she asked, a hint of color touching her cheeks. "Food on my face?"

"No," he said, shaking his head. "Just thinking this is... nice."

"Nice?" she teased, tilting her head. "That's your grand romantic description?"

"I could say perfect, but then you'd think I'm trying too hard."

She leaned forward, eyes glinting with that mix of challenge and warmth that always undid him. "Maybe you already are."

He raised his mug in a toast. "Worth it."

She clinked hers against his, smiling. "We'll see." She sipped her coffee, then added. "Actually, you're not bad company for a guy who insists on plating breakfast like it's a Michelin review."

He chuckled, cutting into his omelet. "Old habits. Presentation's everything."

His phone buzzed. It rattled against the counter, flashing his father's name across the screen. He froze for half a heartbeat. Then, with a quick exhale, he turned the ringer off. "That can wait."

Scarlett arched a brow. "You sure? Could be important."

"Oh, it's important," he said lightly, forcing a grin. "Just not before breakfast."

She studied him, but let any curiosity go, stabbing another bite of omelet instead. "You've got that look again," she said. "Like you're plotting something."

"Plotting," he echoed with a laugh. "More like calculating how to keep my father from turning the restaurant into another Rivera empire outpost."

"Ah. Family business drama before coffee."

He relaxed a little, smiling at her tone. "You make it sound fun."

"Everything's fun if there's hollandaise."

That earned her another grin. But as she took a sip of coffee, he glanced again at the phone. The screen was dark now, but his father's voice echoed anyway—pressure, expectations, the unspoken reminder that this little pocket of peace wouldn't last long.

Still, when Scarlett looked up and smiled at him over her mug, the knot in his chest eased. For a bit longer, the restaurant could wait.

Chapter 17

Over the next few days, the Eclipse Lounge had basically become Scarlett's office. Today, Scarlett sat at the bar, her laptop open, a notebook beside her filled with three neatly drawn columns. Decorations, food, and games. She was so focused, she didn't notice Dante behind her until his breath brushed her shoulder.

"No chocolate fountain?" he murmured, leaning in just enough to read her list.

"I'm planning Rebecca's baby shower, not a Vegas buffet."

He chuckled, sliding onto the stool next to her. "That's a shame. I was starting to look forward to the chocolate."

"You're incorrigible," she teased, bumping his arm lightly before turning back to her list.

He grinned. "That's a fancy word for charming, right?"

She rolled her eyes and looked at him, letting her gaze roam over his face. Even with his hair slightly disheveled from working in the restaurant's hot kitchen all morning, and a shadow of whiskers from not shaving before he'd left the house. He looked wonderful.

"I think you'd look good with a beard. You should let it grow." She ran her fingers along his jaw.

"Yeah?" He took her hand and kissed her palm. "I've always wanted one. It might make me look European."

They laughed.

Scarlett glanced up at him, her pulse doing that ridiculous flutter it had started doing whenever he looked at her that way—like she was the only person in the room. They'd been spending more time together. And even though their relationship seemed to be moving fast, it felt right.

"Enough messing around. I have to get this shower planned."

"Have you decided on the menu?"

"Rebecca wants something light and pretty. Finger foods, mocktails, that sort of thing. I'm thinking mini caprese skewers, lemon tarts, and your smoked salmon crostini. Keep it elegant, not fussy."

"Done," he said easily. "You tell me what you want, I'll make it happen."

He reached across the bar and squeezed her hand, and the simple touch sent a shiver up her arm.

"Where's your friend, Rayna? I thought she wanted to help you?"

"She worked at Mo's last night, then had to do inventory this morning."

"Okay, so can someone else help?" he asked.

Scarlett lifted a brow, amused. "Oh, I'll have plenty of help from my girlfriends. But, honestly, I kind of live for this stuff. Event planning is my thing."

He smirked. "Control freak, got it."

She shot him a mock glare. "I prefer highly organized professional, thank you very much."

She was about to add something else when the front doors swung open, and she heard Dante gasp. Her teasing faded as she turned toward the entrance.

A slender blonde woman stepped inside. Dressed in a short mini shirt, off-the-shoulder white sweater, and knee-high boots with heels at least four inches high, she looked like a supermodel. An uncomfortable wave of dread swept through Scarlett when she started walking toward them.

"Dante," the woman said, voice smooth and polished. "There you are."

He straightened, his smile vanishing as his eyes widened. "Kelly?"

Scarlett's stomach tightened. She knew *that look*. It said history.

Kelly's gaze swept over Scarlett, cool and assessing, before settling back on Dante. "Am I interrupting something?"

"We're planning a baby shower," Dante replied.

"For your baby?" Kelly asked sweetly.

Scarlett's eyebrows lifted. Her gaze snapped to Dante. His expression flickered somewhere between disbelief and dread.

"I'm joking. Relax." The woman's voice was smooth and confident. She turned to Scarlett with a smile full of practiced charm and sophistication. "Dante has always been so literal." Then she stepped closer to him and brushed a kiss on his cheek. "I can wait until you finish your meeting," she added lightly. "I just knew you were missing your *fiancée.*"

The word hit Scarlett like a slap. *Fiancée?*

No, no, no!

"I have to go," she managed, the words cracking in her throat. She didn't wait for an explanation.

Couldn't.

She rushed for the door, every breath burning. Dante called her name, but she kept running. She didn't want to hear his voice, didn't want excuses, didn't want to see his face. What was there to say?

In the parking lot, she fumbled with her keys, climbed into her car, and slammed the door shut. Her hands trembled against the steering wheel. For a moment, she just sat there, chest tight, vision blurred. Then a scream tore out of her, raw and helpless.

God, not again. Please, not again.

* * *

"Scarlett!" he called again, pushing past Kelly.

She didn't turn around. Didn't slow down. By the time he reached the door, she was already in her car.

"Scarlett!" He screamed her name as he raced toward her already moving vehicle. She didn't stop. Tires squealed as she pulled into the street.

He stood there, breath ragged, his pulse pounding in his ears. Of all the ways this could've gone wrong, *this* wasn't supposed to be one of them. He yanked a hand through his hair, anger flashing beneath the confusion, anger, guilt.

Kelly's smirk was waiting when he returned inside.

"What the hell, Kelly?" he demanded. "You've really outdone yourself."

She just shrugged, amused. "Maybe next time, you'll return my calls."

He didn't answer. All he could see was Scarlett and the hurt in her eyes, and the way she'd stormed out as if she'd been burned.

"Nice to see you too," Kelly said, slipping off her sunglasses and perching them on top of her head. "You look good, Dante. Arizona agrees with you."

He exhaled slowly. "Cut it. Why are you here?"

Kelly shrugged, setting her designer bag on the bar like she owned it. "I'm consulting for a resort opening in Scottsdale. When I saw your name in that food critic's blog, I thought, *well, why not stop by?* I didn't expect an audience."

"What were you trying to accomplish with the fiancée stunt?"

Her brows lifted. "Stunt?"

His voice dropped, sharp and low. "You think that's funny?"

Kelly gave a light, dismissive laugh. "Oh, come on. You were the one who called me that more than once, if I remember right."

"A long time ago," he said, jaw tightening. "You know what we had wasn't serious."

She smiled. "You were serious enough when you promised we'd travel together, open a restaurant, start a life."

"Then you ran off with my sous chef."

That shut her up, briefly. She glanced away, smoothing an invisible wrinkle from her dress. "Ancient history."

"Not to the woman who just heard you call yourself my fiancée," he shot back.

Her eyes softened, like she almost pitied him. "Oh. I didn't realize you were with someone special."

"More than you know."

"You really like her, don't you?"

He didn't answer. Didn't need to.

Kelly's expression flickered. Amusement, maybe jealousy, maybe both. "You always did fall too fast."

Dante exhaled, forcing his voice to stay even. "You need to leave, Kelly."

"Fine." She slung her bag over her shoulder and slid on her sunglasses, every motion slow and deliberate. "But don't expect me to be waiting around when you're done with this little fling."

She turned and walked out the same way she'd come—composed, calculated, unapologetic.

The door closed behind her, the echo sharp in the quiet lounge. Joe stood behind the bar, polishing a glass. "Well," he said carefully, "that was... something."

"Don't." Dante's voice came out low, rough. He dragged a hand through his hair and pressed his palms to the edge of the bar, staring at nothing.

He'd thought he'd buried that part of his life when he fell for Scarlett. The chaos, the games, the mess he swore he'd never repeat. But the second Kelly walked in, it was like every mistake he'd ever made was standing in front of him, wearing designer heels and a smug smile.

And now Scarlett had seen it.

The look on her face. The shock, disbelief, and hurt flashed through his mind, and his chest tightened. He'd give anything to take it back, to explain, to fix it. But deep down, he knew words wouldn't touch what Kelly had just wrecked.

He grabbed his keys off the counter and turned for the door. "I gotta find Scarlett," he muttered.

Joe called after him, "Maybe give her a little time."

But the door was already closing behind him.

Chapter 18

Scarlett barely remembered the drive to Rayna's. It was just flashes of traffic lights and the blur of vehicles through her tears. By the time she reached the front door, her hands were shaking so badly she almost dropped her purse.

"Oh, my God, what's wrong?" her friend said when she opened the door and saw the tears pouring down her face.

"He's engaged," she choked out. "It's just like what David did to me." Her words came in a rush, ragged and broken. She threw her arms around Rayna, clinging to her like the ground had disappeared beneath her feet.

"Shit," Rayna whispered. "Come in, tell me what happened."

She stumbled onto the couch, her chest still heaving. "She just...she walked in and called him *fiancée*." She fisted her hands in her lap. "And he didn't deny it. He just sat there, like he didn't know what to say."

Rayna scooted closer beside her, gently rubbing circles on her back. "Oh, honey."

"I can't believe I fell for it again." She pressed the heels of her hands against her eyes, trying to stop the flood. "I told myself I would never again, and then he—" Her voice broke. "He made me believe he was different."

Rayna reached for a box of tissues and handed it to her. "You had every right to believe it. Dante seemed like the real deal."

Scarlett let out a shaky laugh and mentally rolled her eyes. "Yeah, well, apparently his fiancée thought so too."

For a long moment, neither of them spoke. The only sound was Scarlett's whimpering and the faint voices on Rayna's television in the background.

"What am I going to do?" Scarlett wailed.

Rayna sighed and brushed a strand of hair from Scarlett's damp cheek. "You don't have to figure it out today. Just breathe for now."

She nodded weakly, staring at the crumpled tissue in her hand. "I just... don't know how to trust anyone anymore." She grabbed another tissue from the box.

Rayna patted her friend's arm. "Then don't. Not yet."

"I'll never trust a man again." She blew her nose and slumped back against the couch.

"I know, sweety. It feels that way right now." Rayna patted her shoulder gently. "But someday, you'll look back and realize this wasn't the end. It was just a really awful chapter."

Scarlett gave a humorless laugh. "It's a pretty long chapter."

Rayna stood. "You need something warm. Tea, maybe? Or hot chocolate with extra marshmallows." She headed to the kitchen.

"You don't have to fuss over me."

"I'm your friend. It's literally in my job description."

Before long, Rayna returned with two steaming mugs and set one in front of her.

Scarlett's gaze drifted toward the window, where the last traces of daylight faded into soft orange and gray. Her chest tightened. "I was so stupid, Rayna. I let myself believe in him. And now everything's ruined."

"Nothing's ruined," Rayna said gently. "You'll get through this."

"The baby shower is next week. Rebecca's been counting on me, and now..." She trailed off, pressing the tissue to her eyes. "It was supposed to be at Eclipse Lounge."

"Oh," Rayna murmured, realization dawning. "Right."

Scarlett nodded miserably. "I can't walk back in there, Rayna. Not after what happened. I can't even hear his name without wanting to throw up."

Rayna looked thoughtful for a moment, then said softly, "Okay. So, we'll find another place to hold the shower. You've worked miracles with less time before."

"Not like this." Scarlett's voice cracked. Tears started flowing.

Rayna squeezed her hand. "You'll figure it out. You always do."

She gave a slight, defeated nod, but her eyes filled again. "I just wanted it to be perfect for Rebecca. She deserves that. I promised her I'd handle everything."

"We'll find a new venue. You'll spend the night here and let it be about breathing, crying, whatever you need. Tomorrow, we problem-solve."

Scarlett exhaled shakily, wiping her cheeks. "Okay," she whispered, looking down at her cup. "Tomorrow."

* * *

Dante stayed long after close, well past the last server clocking out and Joe killing the lights behind the bar. The silence inside Eclipse felt different tonight. What used to be a satisfying calm after a good shift now felt hollow.

He drifted through the kitchen, checking burners that were already cold, pretending there was still something left to do. But his mind wouldn't let go of Scarlett and how the shock in her eyes gave way to hurt, then disbelief. She'd looked right through him, as if everything between them had been a lie.

He'd gone to her house, but she wasn't there. He'd called more than once, but it went straight to voicemail. He hadn't left a message. What would he say? Kelly was lying? That he hadn't seen her in months and sure as hell hadn't asked her to show up and blow his world apart? Scarlett wouldn't believe him.

He wandered back to the bar and sat down. He blew out a breath and ran his hand through his hair. Glancing up, he caught his reflection in the mirror behind the bottles. His hair looked a mess, his eyes shadowed, his expression wrecked.

"Congratulations, Rivera," he muttered. "You've lost the best thing you ever had."

He sat there as the hours slowly passed, the only sound the hum of the refrigerators.

Dawn was already breaking when his phone buzzed. A text from his father. He didn't bother reading it. For the first time in a long while, he didn't care about business.

All he wanted was one more chance to

make Scarlett believe him.

Chapter 19

Scarlett sat cross-legged on Rayna's couch with her laptop balanced on her knees, phone on speaker, and a headache pulsing just behind her eyes.

"Hi, yes, I'm checking availability for next Saturday afternoon," she said to yet another venue. "A baby shower. Indoors, about thirty guests... oh, you're booked."

She ended the call and dropped her head back against the cushion with a groan. "That's the fourth one."

Rayna handed her a tissue and a cup of coffee. "Fifth. You hung up on the winery before she finished her sentence."

Scarlett sniffed, half-laughing, half-sobbing. "She started with, "Unfortunately." I know how that story ends."

"You could host it here," Rayna offered. "Rebecca won't care if the backdrop is my dining room wall and a few Target balloons."

"I can't do that to her," Scarlett said, voice wobbling. "No offence."

Rayna smirked. "None taken."

Scarlett managed a small laugh, "Thank you."

"I know you want to create something special for her."

"I really do." Scarlett sighed and pressed the tissue to her eyes. "Oh, this is ridiculous. I plan corporate galas for five hundred people. I've pulled off weddings where the bride's mother hated the groom's family. And I can't find one baby shower venue that isn't booked solid."

"You're fine," Rayna said. "You just had the universe dump a bucket of crazy on you."

Scarlett lowered the tissue, her face tightening. "It wasn't the universe. It was me. I let myself get comfortable. I let him get close." She shook her head. "And now his supposed fiancée walks in like she's delivering karma personally."

"You didn't deserve that. Nobody does."

"I should've known better. After David—" Scarlett stopped, the name catching in her throat. "He lied, too. Different details, same humiliation. Guess I've got a type."

"No," Rayna said gently. "You've got a heart. There's a difference."

"Some heart. It's apparently stamped with 'return to sender.'"

"Stop." Rayna nudged Scarlett's foot. "He blindsided you. You didn't pick this."

"Well, I picked the restaurant." She rubbed her temple. "And now I have to call Rebecca and explain why the baby shower isn't happening at the gorgeous new Eclipse Lounge everyone's been raving about."

"So, tell her you changed your mind. She'll believe you."

"I can't lie to her," Scarlett said softly. "I just don't want her feeling bad for me. Not during this exciting time for her."

"You know what? You're still standing." Rayna set her coffee down and leaned back. "You didn't melt down in public, you didn't throw anything, and you're already re-planning. That's more than most people could manage."

"That's because if I stop moving, I'll start thinking, and if I start thinking, I'll lose it."

"Then keep moving. Call Wildflower House again. Offer them your firstborn child if you have to."

"If they say yes, I'm naming the punch after you." Scarlett picked up her phone, the smallest ghost of a smile tugging at her mouth.

"Rayna's Revenge?"

"Exactly."

She started dialing again. Her voice was still unsteady, but her hands didn't shake as much this time. She wasn't sure if it was resolve or exhaustion, but at least it felt like control and right now, that was enough.

* * *

Eclipse Lounge was too quiet.

Not peaceful after closing quiet, more like every sound feels like judgment quiet.

Dante leaned on the bar, watching the ice in his glass melt. He wasn't sure what stung more, the silence or the fact that Scarlett's favorite playlist was still queued up on the sound system. He'd tried changing it earlier, but couldn't bring himself to hit delete.

He wasn't that heartless. Or maybe he just wasn't that brave.

A noise interrupted his thoughts. He looked up. Joe had walked in carrying a box of liquor inventory. "You planning on staring that ice to death, boss? Or are we opening a meditation lounge now?"

Dante exhaled through his nose. "Working on my Zen."

"Looks more like self-pity with better lighting."

"How's the wife?"

Joe set the box down, grunting. "Cheryl's doing better. Ribs are healing, but she'll be wearing a cast on her arm for a long time. Her sister's staying a couple of weeks, so I'm off nurse duty, unless you count keeping her from lifting laundry baskets."

"She's lucky. Getting hit by a red-light runner could have been much worse."

"Don't I know it. Totaled her car."

Dante shook his head. "Tell her I said hi. And to stop sending me pictures of cats in chef hats."

Joe smirked. "Those brighten your day, admit it."

"Sure. Nothing says motivation like a kitten making risotto."

For a moment, it almost felt normal until Joe's gaze drifted toward the end of the bar, where several roses sat drooping in a vase. Dry petals were scattered on the counter. A leftover from one of Scarlett's events.

"You ever gonna throw that out?" Joe asked.

Dante followed his look. "Nope."

Joe nodded. "Didn't think so. You want to talk about it, or you want me to distract you with whiskey and bad advice?"

"Depends. Is your bad advice free?"

"Always. My good advice costs a drink."

Dante smirked, then held up his glass. "Hit me with your best."

Joe refilled the glass and placed it on the bar top. "All right. You and Miss Clipboard had something real. You messed up, she walked. Classic case. But if I've learned anything from ten years of marriage, it's this: women don't stay mad forever."

"She looked pretty committed to the idea," Dante said, half a smile tugging his mouth.

"Yeah, well, so did Cheryl the time I shrunk her favorite sweater in the dryer. Still married."

Dante chuckled. "You're comparing my relationship disaster to a laundry mishap?"

"Hey, both involve heat and poor timing."

That earned an eye roll, but some of the tightness in Dante's chest loosened.

Joe wiped the dead pedals from the counter and tossed them in the trash. "You'll figure it out. Maybe start with an apology that doesn't sound like a business memo."

"I'll keep that in mind."

"Good. Now go on home. I'll close up."

Dante stood, grabbed his keys, and gave the empty room one last glance. "You sure you're good here?"

Joe nodded. "Go. And if you text her, spell-check first. Nothing kills romance faster than 'I miss your face' autocorrected to 'I miss your Mace.'"

Outside, the night air was cool, carrying that faint desert scent of creosote and dust. He turned toward the parking lot and stopped. A folded napkin lay on the ground, one of Scarlett's, her neat handwriting looping across the corner: *Table layout patio option.*

He picked it up, thumb brushing the ink. For a second, he could almost hear her voice again. Confident, teasing, sure of what she wanted.

But the truth pressed in hard. She'd seen Kelly, heard the lies, and walked away without looking back. And no number of words would convince her that he'd never been engaged to Kelly. Not ever.

Dante tucked the napkin into his pocket. Some things, he thought, you didn't throw away no matter how much they hurt to keep.

As he headed for his car, Joe's voice echoed in his head: *"Women don't stay mad forever."*

Dante gave a humorless laugh. "Yeah, Joe," he muttered. "You don't know Scarlett."

Chapter 20

By the time Scarlett pulled into the gravel lot of Desert Bloom Estates, her optimism was hanging by a thread. And that thread was frayed.

"This looks... promising," Rayna said carefully, peering out the passenger window.

Scarlett followed her gaze. The estate's sign, once elegant, now leaned at a dramatic angle, one corner of the wood split from the summer sun. A pair of faded balloons clung to the gate from what looked like last weekend's wedding.

"It's fine," Scarlett said, more to herself than Rayna. "They've hosted events here for years. Besides, it's this or nothing. I've called everywhere twice, begging. This time of year, everyone is booked. I just need to see the space."

"Sure. And the gate's already festive," Rayna muttered.

Scarlett shot her a look but couldn't stop the corner of her mouth from twitching. "Behave."

Once they stepped through the courtyard gate, the mood changed completely. The air smelled faintly of sage and orange blossoms from nearby planters. Golden lantana and trailing rosemary spilled over the edges of the walkway, and the soft burble of a fountain echoed through the open space.

A woman in a wide-brimmed hat came down the pathway, clipboard in hand, with a bright, welcoming smile.

"You must be Scarlett!" she said, extending her hand. "I'm Carla. So nice to meet you."

"Thank you," Scarlett replied, shaking her hand. "This is my friend, Rayna."

Carla greeted Rayna with an easy nod. "Please feel free to look around. If you have any questions, I'll be in the office," she said, gesturing toward a stucco building. "And sorry about the sign out front. We've got a new one coming next week."

Scarlett nodded, scanning the property. The stucco walls glowed honey-gold in the afternoon light, trimmed with desert vines just beginning to turn silver-green in the cooler weather. Beyond the terrace, the foothills rolled toward the mountains, dotted with saguaros and late-blooming brittlebush. Despite her rocky first impression, the place was actually pretty stunning.

Rayna walked to the edge of the patio, brushing her hand along a planter overflowing with lavender and feathery Mexican feather grass. "Okay," she admitted,

"I take it back. This is gorgeous. Like, bridesmaid-group-photo gorgeous."

"See? You just have to look past the leaning sign."

"And the mystery string lights."

"They add character."

Rayna arched a brow. "You and your definition of character."

She ignored her, already imagining tables draped in soft blush linens, string lights glowing above, and candles flickering against terracotta pots filled with desert roses. She could practically hear Rebecca's laugh echoing through the courtyard.

"This has everything we need," she said, turning to her friend.

"Absolutely." Rayna said. "It's got Scottsdale chic written all over it."

Scarlett took one last look at the courtyard, the fading sunlight turning the walls to amber. "Let's go lock it in."

Rayna looped her arm through Scarlett's as they headed for the office. "You found the perfect place. Elegant and drama-free."

Scarlett smirked. "And may it stay that way."

* * *

The lunch rush had faded, leaving Eclipse with that mid-afternoon lull, Quiet music, clinking glassware, and too much room for thinking. Dante sat in his office, working on next week's schedule.

A knock broke the silence. Joe leaned against the doorframe, holding a sheet of paper. "Got something you should see."

Dante looked up. "What now?"

"An email came in from Scarlett."

The sound of her name made his pulse hitch. He straightened. "Really?"

Joe stepped inside and handed him the note the hostess had written. "Canceling the baby shower."

Dante's eyes moved down the words. It was short and polite.

Client says thank you for your time, but they have chosen a different venue. Please release our reservation for the date listed.

He read it twice, as if he might find a trace of her voice between the lines. There wasn't a hint. "She could have done it in person," he said quietly.

Joe shrugged.

Dante leaned back in his chair, the paper rustling between his fingers.

Joe crossed his arms. "Can't blame her for not wanting to come back here."

"I don't," He rubbed his hand over the new hair growing on his jaw. "I just wish she'd told me herself."

"Would you have wanted that conversation?"

Dante paused. "Fair point."

Joe's tone softened. "For what it's worth, I believe you. About Kelly."

"Thanks. Doesn't matter, though. Scarlett saw what she saw."

"Then you show her what's true," Joe said simply. "Actions, not words. And maybe a handwritten apology, women love those."

That earned a chuckle. "You should write a book."

"Already started one. *'A Bartender's Guide to Surviving Marriage'*."

Dante laughed. Then he looked back at the printed email, the clean, emotionless words that somehow said everything.

"She was supposed to do something beautiful here," he murmured. "For her friend."

Joe hesitated. "You're still allowed to want her back, you know."

Dante folded the email and dropped it into the drawer. "Yeah," he said quietly. "Doesn't mean she'll want me."

Chapter 21

Monday morning should've felt like victory.

Scarlett sat across from her boss, sunlight streaming through the floor-to-ceiling windows of Gala Elegance's downtown office. Her presentation folders were perfectly aligned, her blazer pressed, her smile professional. It was the kind of moment she'd imagined for years. The payoff for late nights, impossible clients, and the stubborn belief that hard work would eventually speak louder than luck.

"Scarlett," her boss said, sliding a cream-colored envelope across the desk. "You've earned this. The Event Director Coordinator position is officially yours, and you are now a partner with the firm. Congratulations."

The words should've hit like champagne bubbles. Exhilarating, effervescent, worth every ounce of effort.

But instead, the sound echoed in her chest like an empty glass.

"Thank you," she managed, her voice steady even as something inside her cracked. She forced a smile, accepted the handshake, and said all the right things. Grateful, humbled, excited. She even laughed in the right places.

When the meeting ended, she walked out into the hall clutching the envelope like it was the one thing holding her together. The office buzzed with the usual Monday rhythm, phones ringing, printers humming, snippets of conversation drifting through open doors.

Usually, she loved that energy. Today, it just made her feel tired.

Rayna met her near the elevators, eyes wide. "Well?"

"It's official." Scarlett held up the envelope.

"Yes!" Rayna squealed and pulled her into a hug. "Finally! You've worked your butt off for this."

"I know. It's... surreal."

Rayna pulled back, studying her face. "Then why do you look like someone just told you they canceled Christmas?"

Scarlett exhaled. "Because I thought getting the promotion was my dream."

Rayna tilted her head. "And?"

She laughed softly. "I have everything I thought I wanted. But all I can think about is how I wish I could tell...you know who...him."

"You can still tell him."

Scarlett shook her head. "No. That's over and done. My choice."

"That's probably the right choice," Rayna said. "But, it doesn't make it easy."

Scarlett looked out the window, where the desert skyline stretched wide and bright. From up here, everything looked small: the streets, the buildings, even her problems. But her chest still ached, a slow, dull pulse that didn't match the brightness outside.

"This is supposed to be a good day," she whispered.

"It still is," Rayna said. "You just haven't caught up to it yet."

"Maybe that's it." Scarlett smiled faintly, blinking back tears she refused to let fall.

As she stepped into the elevator, the envelope still in her hand, she told herself she'd get there eventually. That the sting would fade, that her heart would stop reacting every time someone said his name.

But deep down, she already knew the truth. You can get everything you ever wanted and still feel like you lost the one thing that mattered most.

* * *

A glance across the dining room told Dante everything he needed to know. Tables turned smoothly, servers smiled, and guests were content. Drinks were flowing, no delays. In the kitchen, orders were plated at the perfect time, hot and artfully garnished. Nights like this, when everything ran seamlessly, when the chaos stayed invisible, that was when he remembered why he loved this work.

It should've been satisfying.

So why did it all feel flat?

Joe stepped closer, bar rag over his shoulder. "Busy night. We might actually sell out of the duck special before nine. You can stop brooding now."

"I'm not brooding."

Joe arched a brow. "You're staring at a salt shaker like it owes you money. That's peak brooding."

Dante shrugged.

Joe filled a glass with soda water and gave it to him. After a second, he spoke, "Cheryl showed me something earlier. That company Scarlett works for posted about her promotion on social media."

Dante stilled. "Promotion?"

"Yeah. Looks like she's doing real well."

He forced a nod. "I'm glad for her."

"She earned it," Joe said. "The woman could run the Super Bowl with a paperclip and a Post-it note."

"Yeah," Dante murmured, eyes drifting toward the far wall. "She always made chaos look easy."

For a moment, neither spoke. The music shifted to a mellow jazz track Scarlett had added to the playlist months ago. Dante considered skipping it, but he couldn't bring himself to move.

"She deserves everything good that happens to her," he said finally.

Joe gave him a sidelong glance. "Well, for what it's worth, you don't look half as miserable as you did last week. That's progress."

"Don't set the bar too high."

Joe chuckled, then moved to greet a couple who'd just sat down at the end of the bar.

Dante stayed where he was, watching the reflection of the room in the mirror behind the bottles, glasses sparkling, lights soft, everything in its place. It should have felt like success. But all he could think was how only a few weeks ago Scarlett had stood right there, adjusting flowers, laughing at him for being too serious.

He turned away, forcing a breath. She was gone. She was moving on. And it was time he did the same.

At least, that's what he kept telling himself.

Chapter 22

Dante didn't notice the black Mercedes parked in front of the Eclipse Lounge until he caught Joe's expression. The bartender froze mid-pour, then gave a low whistle. "Well, look who just blew in."

He turned toward the entrance to see Julian Rivera step inside like he owned the place, which, technically, he did. The older man looked polished as ever, his dark gray pinstripe suit, his gold cufflinks catching the light as he slid off his sunglasses.

"Hey," Dante said as he stood to grab his dad's outstretched hand. "What is this, a surprise inspection?"

Immediately, their handshake turned into a genuine hug.

Julian pulled back and gave a bright smile. "Besides missing my boy, I have interesting news."

Seeing Joe, he lifted his hand. "Joe, good to see you."

"You too, boss. Can I fix your regular?"

"Sound good." Then, turning to Dante, he gestured toward a table near the window. "Sit. We need to talk."

Must be interesting to come all the way to Arizona, he thought as he followed his dad to the table.

Once they were seated, Julian didn't bother with small talk. "I've been watching what you've done here. The numbers and the reviews. I didn't think you'd pull it off this soon, but you did."

"Is that... a compliment?"

There was a glint of pride in his father's eyes. "Absolutely. You've proven you can manage more than a menu. That's what I needed to see."

Dante leaned back, wary. "Okay. What's this leading to?"

"New York, son." He slid a folder across the table. "New York."

Dante's eyebrows lifted as he opened the folder. Inside was a set of plans, elegant renderings of a Manhattan dining room with sleek lighting and marble floors, the kind of place food critics called visionary.

"I'm opening a new flagship in New York," Julian said. "The Rivera Group's crown jewel." He leaned forward. "I want you to run it."

"You're serious?"

"Completely. You'll be the executive director. Your name on the front, full creative control. And if it goes well..." Julian paused, a smile tugging his mouth. "I'm thinking of an international expansion. Paris."

The words landed like a gut punch. This was everything Dante had worked for: respect, recognition, and the chance to stand beside his father instead of in his shadow.

"What do you say?"

Joe interrupted by setting a scotch onto the table, allowing Dante a moment to process the question.

Julian thanked Joe, took a sip, and turned his attention to Dante.

At this moment, he should have jumped for joy, but all he could think of was not being able to tell Scarlett.

He cleared his throat. "Do you need my answer now?"

That surprised his dad. "I was expecting you to be more excited. What's going on?"

"Nothing. I'm just caught off guard. When do I need to be in New York?"

Julian checked his watch. "The investors are coming next week. I want to introduce you personally. That is, if you're sure you're ready to step up."

"I've always been ready," Dante said automatically.

His father nodded, clearly pleased. "Good. My assistant will send you the details. And Dante..." He hesitated. "I'm proud of you. And your mother will be happy to have you close again." He stood. "My turnaround flight leaves soon. I'll see you, son."

As quickly as he arrived, Julian was gone.

Dante sat for a long moment, staring at the life-changing papers. He ran a thumb along the edge of the folder, as if feeling the weight of what it meant. A bigger stage. Recognition. All the things he'd told himself he wanted.

He leaned back in the chair, glancing around the restaurant he'd built from scratch. Every detail bore Scarlett's touch. The layout she'd fought for, the amber light she'd insisted would make guests linger longer, even the floral accents she'd argued weren't too much. And the patio. It was completed now, and he had to admit, she'd been right, of course. Arizona clientele loved being outside, especially in the fall weather.

He exhaled, low and uneven. Rubbing the back of his neck, he whispered, "How did my life become so complicated?"

"Talking to yourself again?" Joe's voice interrupted his mumbling.

"Old habit," Dante said. He pushed back the chair, stood, grabbed the folder, and walked to the bar.

Joe joined him. "Your dad gone already?"

"Yeah." Dante tapped the folder. "New York. Wants me to run his flagship restaurant. Maybe Paris after that."

Joe whistled softly. "That's big."

"Yeah." He gave a faint, tired smile. "It's everything I thought I wanted."

"But?"

Dante hesitated. "I don't know. It just feels...final. Like, once I go, that's it."

Joe studied him for a moment, then nodded. "Maybe that's what you need. Clean break. New view. Different ghosts."

"Maybe."

They stood there in companionable silence for a moment. Joe finally spoke again. "You've got nothing holding you here, right?"

Dante swallowed hard. "No," he said. "Nothing is keeping me here anymore." He straightened, pushing the folder under his arm. "Guess I should start planning my move. You can lock up."

Joe gave him a look that was equal parts pride and sympathy. "Just don't forget us small-town folks when you're sipping espresso in Paris."

Dante managed a grin. "Wouldn't dream of it."

But as he walked toward the door, the smile faded. Outside, the night stretched wide and quiet, the air scented faintly with desert sage. He paused at the edge of the patio, staring out toward the mountains where the last light of day faded into indigo.

For the first time, the future was wide open. And somehow, it never felt emptier.

Chapter 23

The baby shower for Rebecca came together exactly the way Scarlett planned. She scanned the tables one last time. The centerpieces looked lovely, and fluffy bunny and baby fox decorations were everywhere. Perfection.

Friends began to arrive, arms full of pastel wrapped gifts and enough ribbon to stock a craft store. The mom-to-be positively glowed, her smile lighting up the sunny afternoon. The caterers were in full swing, setting out trays of chicken-salad croissants, bite-sized sliders, pasta primavera, and a Mediterranean grain salad that looked too good to eat. Dessert was a cupcake tower, lemon, strawberry, and vanilla with swirls of pastel frosting.

The afternoon unfolded in a blur of laughter, photos, and pink-and-blue chaos. Guests cheered as gifts were opened, and when the last cupcake vanished and the sugar rush hit, chatter grew louder, and the guests were ready for the games to begin.

"Okay, everyone," Rayna announced, clapping her hands with mock authority.

"Time for the guess what the baby food is game?"

Groans and giggles erupted. Trisha covered her face. "Please tell me this doesn't involve actual baby food."

Rayna laughed and handed her a spoon. "Oh, it absolutely does. Don't worry, I labeled the mystery jars alphabetically. It's all very scientific."

"You're evil," Trisha groaned, but her grin gave her away.

It was party perfect, until the sound of two servers chatting near the buffet caught Scarlett's ear. She wasn't trying to eavesdrop. but their voices carried.

"Did you get your schedule for the new place yet?" one girl asked, stacking glasses.

"Yes," the other replied. "I start next week. It will be better for me. Evening shift, regular hours."

"Oh, I get that," the first girl said. "Besides, I hear the Eclipse Lounge manager is ridiculously good-looking."

"His name is Dante, but he's going back to New York. Too bad because he's an amazing chef."

Scarlett swallowed hard and pretended to fuss with the silverware, though her chest had gone tight. *New York*. Of course. Why wouldn't he be? That world was his. Fine dining, high stakes, beautiful women. Someone like Kelly.

Kelly.

She could still see her walking into Eclipse, with perfect hair and effortless confidence, looking at Dante.... Stop. You don't care. She inhaled deeply, in, out, in, out.

Rayna's voice snapped her back. "Scarlett, you're up next. Guess the baby food flavor."

"Right," she blinked, forcing a smile. "Bring it on," she said brightly.

Everyone roared with laughter at her silly expressions as someone filmed the moment for posterity. Rebecca's mom, Olivia, cheered from the sidelines, and even the caterers abandoned their trays to see what the commotion was about.

"This," Trisha said, coming up beside her, "is what all your late nights are for.

"Worth it, huh?" Rayna added.

Scarlett nodded, her throat a little tight. "Yeah. Totally worth it."

By late afternoon, the party was winding down. Rayna was helping Rebecca and her mom load all the gifts into her SUV. Trisha was wrangling a rogue cluster of balloons that refused to fit through the door.

Sinking into one of the white folding chairs, she let her shoulders slump for the first time all day. The tablecloths were wrinkled now, petals scattered like confetti across the grass. She stared at them, unfocused.

New York. Dante. She let out a low laugh. "Should've known better."

She sat for another minute, then went back to work. She boxed up the last vase and stepped back, surveying the picture-perfect patio one final time. The area was spotless, the tables gleamed, chairs stacked neatly, and no one would guess the planner behind it all felt like she'd been sucker-punched.

"Perfect day," she muttered to no one. "Too bad my love life didn't get the memo."

* * *

Dante leaned against the bar, staring at the half-empty glass in front of him. The lounge was quiet now. The servers, the chefs, even Joe had already clocked out. Everything was quiet.

He took a slow sip, letting the whiskey burn its way down before settling warm in his chest. *New York*. It should've felt like good news. His father had called earlier, his voice full of excitement about the opportunity. His mother had chimed in, thrilled he'd be home for good before Christmas. They were already planning parties, no doubt inviting half of Manhattan to celebrate his success.

So why did it feel like failure?

Dante set his glass down, the sound sharp against the counter. The deal in New

York was supposed to be a step forward, proof that he could stand on his own. But the thought of walking away now and leaving the Eclipse Lounge, leaving *her,* felt like losing more than he was gaining.

He pulled out his phone, thumb hovering over Scarlett's number. He'd almost deleted it once, telling himself it was for the best. But he hadn't. Her name was still there. He wanted to call. To hear her voice. To explain. To say that Kelly didn't mean anything.

Instead, he locked the screen and shoved the phone into his pocket.

He couldn't fix it tonight. Maybe he couldn't fix it at all.

He grabbed his jacket and switched off the bar lights. The lounge went dark, except for the glow spilling in from the city beyond the glass, a reminder that the world kept moving, even when you wished it wouldn't.

Chapter 24

The city skyline came into view just as the plane dipped through a bank of clouds, all glass and glitter against the dark winter sky. Dante expected to feel something: nostalgia, pride, maybe even happiness to be home. Instead, he just felt empty.

The car waiting outside JFK was sleek, black, and predictably chauffeured. His father's idea, of course. He climbed in and watched the city blur by in a wash of headlights and billboards, the December chill frosting the edges of every window. People hurried along the sidewalks, bundled in coats and purpose. This was home. At least, it used to be.

When the car pulled up in front of his parents' estate, the heavy oak entrance door flew open before the driver could even shut off the engine. His mother stood there beaming, her red scarf askew and her eyes already misty.

"Look at you!" she cried, meeting him on the walkway and pulling him into a hug that nearly knocked the air from his lungs. "You're too thin. Didn't you take time to eat in Arizona?"

He laughed softly. "You'd love it there, Mom. Sunshine, great food, less traffic—"

"You're home now. That's what matters," his father interrupted, stepping into the doorway. "Let him come inside," he told his mother.

The house smelled of roasted rosemary chicken and fresh bread. Everything gleamed, polished within an inch of its life. Immediately, he noticed the table was set for six, though only the two of them lived here.

"Some friends are dropping by later," his mother said, fluttering around him. "A little celebration."

Dante smiled politely and reached for the wine on the counter.

By the time the doorbell rang, Dante already knew who it would be.

Monica, his mother's best friend, swept in first, all sleek black dress and red lipstick, air-kissing both of his cheeks. "Dante, back from the desert! Tell me, was it unbearable or just unbearably charming?"

"A little of both," he said with a grin that didn't quite reach his eyes.

Then came longtime family friends, the Whitmores, dripping wealth and holiday cheer, already talking about how they "couldn't wait" to dine at the new Manhattan location.

He smiled, nodded, and poured drinks while the room filled with laughter that didn't quite sound real.

For the first time, Dante realized he'd come home to people who wanted to celebrate his success, not understand his heart.

They talked through dinner about the restaurant deal, the investors, and the future expansion to Paris. His father's eyes lit up at every mention of profit margins and press buzz. Dante nodded, offered practiced enthusiasm, and tried not to picture the twinkling lights strung across the Eclipse Lounge patio or the way Scarlett laughed when something didn't go to plan.

"Everyone's excited you're back," his father said, pouring himself another glass. "This is where you belong. You've always been a New York man."

Dante lifted his glass but didn't drink. "Maybe," he said quietly. "But I'm not sure the city feels the same."

His mother reached over and squeezed his hand. "You're just tired, darling. Once you get back into the swing of things, you'll feel it again."

He smiled at her warmth but knew she was wrong. The city buzzed outside like it always had, but the noise didn't reach him. Not really.

Later that night, alone in the guest bedroom, which was once his childhood room, he stared out the window at the skyline. Somewhere beneath all that glass and ambition, people were falling in love, fighting, chasing dreams just like they always did. And yet, all he could think of was one woman standing, arms crossed, giving him that exasperated half-smile she used whenever he pushed too hard.

He could still hear her voice. *"You're impossible, Dante Rivera."*

He huffed a quiet laugh, rubbing a hand over his jaw. "Yeah," he murmured to the empty room, "and you're unforgettable."

The city might never sleep, but tonight, it didn't matter. Because for the first time, he didn't feel like part of it. He just felt like a man who'd left something real behind.

* * *

"Hi, Rebecca," Scarlett said as her friend opened the front door. The minute she stepped inside the condo, the scent of cinnamon and fresh pine filled her senses. A tree twinkled in the corner, lights reflecting off silver ribbons and sentimental ornaments that looked like they'd each been handpicked.

"You're ready for the holidays early," she commented, glancing around the room.

"I don't want to take any chances." Rebecca patted her protruding tummy. "Could happen sooner than we expect."

"Good idea," she said, noticing how much bigger she was than a few days ago. "Here, I brought you something." She handed her a mason jar filled with peppermint cocoa mix left over from a craft party, and a sparkly ornament shaped like a baby fox, because Rebecca's nursery theme was woodland chic.

"Thank you." She took the gifts. "Come sit down."

They moved to the sofa and spent the next half hour chatting and laughing.

Finally, Scarlett stood. "As much as I hate to go," she reached for her jacket, "I have work to do."

"Don't think about running off yet," Rebecca said. "I need your help."

"Of course. Help with what? You already have enough cookies baked to feed the neighborhood."

"Not cookies. Something better." Rebecca's blue eyes brightened as she reached for a folder on the coffee table. "It's a charity fundraising event for the Haven of Peace women's shelter. I'm on the planning committee."

Scarlett's hand paused midair, still holding her jacket. "Rebecca..."

"I know, you're busy, but you're so good at this. You make things beautiful. And this one actually matters."

The concern in her friend's voice sent a wave of love through her. She'd visited that shelter with Rebecca once, delivering supplies. She could still picture the murals painted by the kids, the comfortable but worn couches, the faces of women trying to start over.

Curiosity softening her resistance, she blew out a breath and sat back down. "So, when's the event?"

"December fifteenth."

"That's only three weeks away," Scarlett blurted.

"Yes," she sighed, then offered a hopeful smile. "Which is why we need a miracle worker. You, specifically."

"Why did you wait so long to ask me?" she asked, her brain already calculating all the steps involved to pull an event like this off.

"I thought I could do it myself. She pressed her lips together. "But now I'm worried I might go into labor, and as happy as that would make me, I could let a bunch of deserving people down." She grinned, leaning forward. "The theme is *A Season of Hope*. We want something elegant but heartwarming. Maybe white and gold? Simple décor. You'd make it perfect. Please."

Scarlett let out a breath, already imagining centerpieces with winter greenery, strings of fairy lights, maybe frosted glass candleholders. "You're really not giving me a choice, are you?"

"Not even a little," Rebecca said cheerfully.

"Fine. I'll do it. But only because I can't stand the idea of you trying to staple garland to the ceiling."

Rebecca gasped in mock offense. "Hey. I could use tape."

They both laughed.

"Thank you," Rebecca said after a moment. "You're really helping a lot of people with this."

She pulled a notepad from her handbag to jot down a few ideas. "Let's make it a night to remember. Fingers crossed you'll be there instead of the maternity ward."

Chapter 25

The sky darkened outside the Riveras' home, cloudy and cold. Dante stood by the window, hands in his pockets, staring into space. Somewhere out there, chefs were shouting, pans were flying, and people were doing what he used to love, creating something that mattered.

He'd thought coming back to New York would feel like slipping into his old skin. Instead, it itched.

"The meeting is confirmed for Friday," his father said from behind his massive desk, scanning a thick stack of papers. "Investors are eager to meet. They love the Paris expansion idea."

"Yeah," Dante muttered. "Great."

His father looked up. "Try to sound like it."

Dante forced a half smile. "Sorry. Long day."

Julian Rivera frowned, setting the papers aside. "You used to light up talking about new projects. What happened?"

Dante's jaw tightened. *She happened.* He shrugged instead. "I'm just tired."

His father leaned back in the high-backed leather chair. "Tired is for people who don't have drive. You've wanted this since culinary school."

"I wanted *freedom*," Dante said quietly. "Not to spend my life chasing the next approval."

"Excuse me?"

But before he could answer, his mother's voice floated in from the doorway. "Are you two at it again?"

Elena Rivera entered the study carrying a tray of espresso cups, her expression the same calm authority that had diffused a thousand father-son battles. "What did I interrupt?"

"Nothing." They both answered at the same time.

She set the tray on the coffee table, then gave her son a stern look. "You've been walking around like a ghost since you got back. You eat, you work, you stare out the window. If this is the dream you wanted, why do you look so miserable living it?"

He rubbed a hand over his jaw. "It's complicated."

"Her name's Scarlett, isn't it?" she asked, her eyes searching his face.

"Who told you that?" Yearning bubbled within him, hearing her name, but he tried to maintain his composure. Act like it didn't matter.

"Joe," she said simply. "He called to check in. Said Arizona was good for you."

His father groaned. "*This* is what's bothering you? A woman?"

"Don't," His mother shot his father a warning look.

Dante stared at the dark surface of his espresso. "She's not just a woman, Mom. She made me happy. I walked away because of a misunderstanding." Then he turned and met his father's glare. "And because I was taught a successful business is what's important."

"What's wrong with me wanting you to be your best?" His father's tone had softened, but only slightly.

"Nothing," Dante said, voice rough. "Except I spent my whole life trying to be *your* best. Maybe it's time I figure out what mine looks like."

Silence stretched between them.

Finally, his mother reached over and touched his arm. "Then go find her."

Julian's head snapped toward her. "Elena—"

"Julian," she cut him off. "You can build a dozen restaurants, but you can't build happiness for your son. He has to do that himself."

Dante blinked, his throat tightening. "Mom, she's done with me."

She smiled softly. "You always had your father's fire. But you have my heart. Don't waste either of them being afraid."

For the first time in weeks, something in his chest shifted.

He stood, kissed his mother's cheek, and turned to leave.

"What are you doing?" His father called after him, exasperated. "We have dinner reservations tonight."

"Something I should've already done," Dante said, heading for the door. He glanced back with a faint grin. "Don't worry. I'll bring you both a souvenir from Arizona."

The door closed behind him, leaving his father muttering and his mother smiling.

Outside, the cold bit through his coat as he stepped into the night. The city lights blurred as a cab splashed past, but for the first time since he'd left Cave Creek, Dante felt warm.

He had no idea what he'd say when he saw her again. He just knew he couldn't leave things unfinished. The city might have built him, but it wasn't home. Home was a woman with fire in her eyes, and he had to make her believe she was the only one who ever had a claim on his heart.

Chapter 26

The plane banked over the desert just as dawn cracked the horizon. A soft orange glow spread across the sky, the kind of color that didn't exist anywhere but Arizona. Dante pressed his hand to the window, squinting against the light.

The captain's voice came over the intercom, cheerful and detached. "Welcome to Phoenix. Local time is six forty-two a.m., and the temperature's a comfortable sixty-five degrees."

Comfortable. Sure. His stomach felt anything but.

He'd spent the flight rehearsing what to say. Every version sounded worse than the last. *I'm sorry* felt too small. *I miss you* felt too selfish. And *I love you*...well, he wasn't sure she'd even let him get that far.

When the plane touched down, he released a breath he hadn't realized he was holding. He'd been running toward this moment since his mother told him to stop being afraid. Now he just had to hope Scarlett hadn't moved on.

An hour later, he'd rented a car at Sky Harbor and headed north. The city unfurled around him in familiar rhythms, palm trees, stucco plazas, morning joggers, and the shimmer of sunlight off glass buildings. The Southwest hadn't changed. He had.

By the time he pulled into the small parking lot behind Eclipse Lounge, the sun was fully up, spilling gold across the patio he and Scarlett had argued over for weeks. The place looked perfect. Lights still strung from the last event, tables stacked neatly, not a detail out of place.

Joe's pickup was parked at an angle, and sure enough, the man was behind the bar when Dante stepped inside.

Joe looked up, eyebrows rising. "Well, surprise, surprise."

"Morning to you, too," Dante said, sliding onto a stool.

Joe poured him a cup of coffee without asking if he wanted one.

He took a sip of the dark brew and grimaced. "You always make it this strong?"

"You're the first to complain." He returned the pot to the warmer, then asked, "What project brings you back so soon?"

"I'm not here on business this time." Dante ran his hand over the back of his neck.

Joe's face softened. "Scarlett?"

He exhaled. "You heard from her lately?"

"Sure. She's been busy. She's hosting a black-tie charity event for the women's shelter Rebecca volunteers at."

Dante's pulse kicked up. "When?"

"Tonight."

"Do you know where it's at?"

"Casa del Sol. Are you thinking about showing up?"

"I don't know, Joe. You think she'd talk to me?"

Joe leaned on the counter. "You've got two choices. Save yourself the heartache and always wonder, or you can go get the girl."

Well, he could damn sure try.

Dante stood up. "I've got to go," he told Joe, then swallowed the last of his coffee. "I've got a tux to rent."

* * *

Scarlett exhaled. It had all come together. Somehow.

The ballroom of Casa del Sol sparkled like winter itself, elegant and full of quiet joy. Guests mingled in sequined dresses and black tuxes, laughter mingling with the scent of cinnamon punch and evergreen. Across the room, a string quartet eased into a soft rendition of *Have Yourself a Merry Little Christmas*. And in the corner of the room next to a beautifully decorated Christmas tree, one of the shelter residents was reading a story to a group of children.

"Scarlett!" Rebecca's voice carried across the room, cheerful and a little breathless as she waddled toward her, glowing in a pale-blue maternity gown that shimmered under the lights.

Scarlett met her halfway, laughing. "Don't run, you'll start a panic. People will think the baby's coming early."

Rebecca grinned. "At least we'd have a great crowd for it. Half the city's here."

Scarlett had to agree as she glanced around the room. The mayor's wife chatted with a local news anchor, even a sports legend, and his wife lingered near the silent-auction table. "I'm just glad no one's allergic to eucalyptus. I used it on practically every centerpiece."

"Are you kidding? Everyone's too distracted by the fabulous dessert bar to notice."

"That's because I bribed the pastry chef. You're welcome."

Rebecca looped her arm through Scarlett's, giving her a gentle squeeze. "You're incredible, you know that? Look at this place, it's stunning. I knew you'd pull it off."

She smiled at her friend, knowing she was laying it on thick since she'd volunteered her services for the shelter. "It's a beautiful venue, Rebecca. You should raise a lot of money for the shelter."

Rebecca chuckled. "Stop being so modest. You're in your element. Admit it. You love this."

"I do," Scarlett said softly. And she meant it. For the first time in weeks, she wasn't thinking about what she'd lost or who she'd walked away from. She was just... here. Surrounded by laughter, candlelight, and something that felt a lot like joy.

A volunteer waved her over from the check-in table. "Scarlett, do you have a moment? We're short a few auction paddles."

"On it," she replied. Then, smoothing her dress, she told Rebecca. "Promise me you'll go sit down and not try to do too much. There are other volunteers."

"Yes, ma'am," her friend teased, then added, "But only if you promise to come keep me company."

"I'll try," she said. "But no guarantees."

The quartet transitioned into *Silver Bells*, and a burst of applause followed. Scarlett was halfway across to the auction table when a deep, booming *"Ho, ho, ho!"* rolled through the room. Heads turned. Children squealed as a man in a red velvet suit appeared in the doorway, waving both hands like he was entering a parade.

She blinked. "Oh no. No, no, no—"

Rebecca yelled, "Surprise!"

Scarlett turned slowly. "Tell me you did *not* recruit your husband for this."

"Who else was I going to get? The professional Santa bailed on me yesterday."

"And you thought Mick was the solution?"

Completely unbothered, she replied, "He looks good with a beard and wearing red."

"I also can see he's been enjoying the cravings right along with you."

Rebecca laughed. "Hey, it's called sympathy weight. He's just being supportive."

As if on cue, *Santa Mick* adjusted his fake belly on his own good-sized frame and called out, "Merry Christmas, everyone! Who's been good this year?"

A chorus of giggles erupted as a dozen kids, all dressed in their Holiday finery, rushed forward, shrieking with joy. Mick ho-ho-ho'd like his life depended on it, his cowboy boots peeking out under the velvet trousers.

Surprised to see Mick wearing anything except his usual biker boots, Scarlett stated softly, "He's wearing Western boots."

Rebecca's expression screamed mischief. "Authentic Arizona Santa."

Mick knelt to hand out candy canes, smiling at Scarlett as she approached. "You're welcome. Mrs. Claus said you needed backup."

Scarlett folded her arms, trying not to laugh. "You realize you're supposed to start *after* the auction, right?"

"Couldn't wait," he chirped. "This suit's about ten degrees too warm, and the beard is synthetic torture."

"Fine. Just try to stay near the Christmas tree. And no impromptu karaoke, we have a band."

"No promises." He winked, then turned to scoop up a squealing toddler, his jolly laugh echoing off the walls.

Rebecca leaned close, whispering, "See? Adorable. Admit it."

"I admit nothing," she answered, but the smile tugging at her mouth betrayed her.

A small crowd of kids surrounded Santa Mick, their laughter spilling through the room as he tried to keep up with candy-cane requests. Rebecca was glowing, and the rest of the guests looked more entertained than annoyed. The photographer hurried over, camera clicking steadily, and Scarlett smiled. The auction could wait a few minutes. For the first time all night, she felt something she hadn't in a long time—content.

Chapter 27

Dante spent the day in a hotel, restless and pacing the room. He'd tried to relax by turning on the TV or scrolling through his emails, but every time he sat still, he saw Scarlett's face. The way she'd looked at him when Kelly called herself his fiancée.

With a sigh of frustration, he headed out to grab a coffee, thinking some air and caffeine would help clear his mind. He walked for blocks, grabbed a sandwich he didn't taste, and rehearsed what he'd say to her. But every version fell apart before he finished.

Back in his room, Dante showered, shaved, and dressed. The routine steadied him, the warm water, a clean shirt, black dress pants, polished shoes, but it didn't quiet the storm inside. He caught his reflection in the mirror, jaw tense, the skin under his eyes darkened. He drew a breath and picked up his keys. There was no perfect speech, no easy fix. All he could do was show up and hope she didn't turn away.

The valet stand at Casa del Sol glittered under a canopy of string lights. He sat in the rental car for a minute before getting out.

His heart thudded hard enough to make his chest ache. *You've survived Michelin critics and your father's lectures. You can survive this.*

Inside, the ballroom pulsed with conversation and music. The kind of event where servers glided, the donors smiled too widely, and everything smelled faintly of money and champagne. He knew instantly it was one of Scarlett's. The soft lighting, the warm color palette, the effortless balance of elegance and ease.

Then he saw her.

Across the room, Scarlett moved through the crowd with a smile as she spoke to a couple near the dessert table. She looked composed and confident. For a split second, he thought about turning around and walking out. Just save himself the humiliation of what he was sure would happen.

But then a tray slipped from one of the servers' hands, sending glasses tumbling toward the floor. Dante moved before he could think. He caught the tray, steadied it, and offered a calm, "Got it," before the server even processed what had happened. Then he straightened, and there she was, looking right at him.

The world seemed to still.

Her lips parted slightly, and her eyes widened, showing confusion that flickered into disbelief.

"Scarlett, they're about to start the presentation," someone called to her.

She smiled and nodded to the woman. Then, without saying a word to him, she turned her back and crossed to the other side of the room.

A slideshow flickered to life on the screen. Photos of the shelter, the women and children it served, and the volunteers who kept the doors open year-round. Applause rose as her friend Rebecca stepped to the podium and took the microphone.

"Tonight is about giving hope a place to grow," she said. "Thanks to all of you and your generous contributions, Haven of Peace will continue to help women start new lives. I also want to thank my dear friend Scarlett Collins. She put this wonderful event together in a very short time. Please give her a round of applause."

Scarlett graciously smiled as the crowd turned toward her, clapping. He wished he could stand by her side and congratulate her as well, but he didn't want to make her more uncomfortable than he already had by just being there.

Staying was pointless. Dante turned toward the exit, the laughter, clinking glasses, and music blurring together as he walked toward the door. He stepped into the courtyard and took a breath of the cool desert air, a sharp contrast to the warmth inside. Hands deep in his pockets, he continued along the stone path. He told himself that leaving was the right call. Scarlett didn't want him there. She was clearly doing fine. He was halfway across the courtyard when he heard footsteps behind him. The soft, quick rhythm of high heels on stone.

"Hey."

He knew her voice instantly. He turned, and there she was, under the twinkling lights, her hair shining, her dress sparkling. For a heartbeat, he couldn't move. Couldn't breathe. She looked unreal, like some holiday illusion he'd conjured up by wishing.

She crossed her arms. "So, you weren't going to say goodbye?"

He shrugged and managed to give her a weak smile. "Didn't think I rated one."

"Please. You've never been short on confidence."

"Guess New York knocked some of that out of me."

For a moment, neither of them said anything. The night felt still, except for the drift of *Silver Bells* from the ballroom. Then, from behind them, Santa's booming "Ho ho ho!" and the kids' laughter echoed through the courtyard. Scarlett's lips twitched like she was fighting a smile.

"Rebecca's idea," she said, tilting her head toward the silly Conga line of kids being led by Santa. "It's Mick. She insisted that he do it. Claimed he already had the belly for it."

Dante chuckled. "He's putting on sympathy weight?"

"Rebecca says it's solidarity."

He nodded, watching the way her eyes lit when she talked about her friends. She looked happy. Or at least she'd gotten good at faking it. He swallowed and asked as casually as possible, trying to forget this could be their last meeting, "Shouldn't you be inside running the show?"

Her chin lifted slightly. "I saw you leaving."

He wasn't sure what to say to that. "I probably shouldn't have crashed your party," he admitted, then he added, "but I'm glad I did. The place looks incredible."

Her expression softened, and she actually smiled. "You always were good at compliments."

"Not flattery," he said. "Just facts."

Silence stretched between them. For a moment, she seemed almost comfortable standing there with him, the faint scent of pine and candle smoke drifting through the courtyard. Then she drew in a quiet breath and stepped back, putting just enough space between them to make her point. And just like that, he knew, the part of her he'd broken couldn't be easily fixed.

He wanted to tell her he'd tried to get used to New York again. That he'd done everything his father asked, smiled for every investor, played the part. But no matter how polished the city looked, something vital was missing. *She* was missing. But instead, he said quietly, "I thought if I came tonight and saw you, maybe I'd finally stop thinking about what we had."

Her breath caught, barely audible, but he heard it.

For a long beat, she just looked at him, eyes searching his face like she wasn't sure whether to believe him... or whether she wanted to. Then she blinked, and the distance was back. The polite, professional calm he'd once admired.

Her voice was steady when she finally spoke. "You don't get to say things like that, Dante. Not after everything."

The words weren't cruel, but they landed like a punch to his gut. He opened his mouth, ready to explain. To tell her Kelly had meant nothing, that there'd never been an engagement, that was all just a stupid misunderstanding.

The ballroom door swung open, spilling warmth and laughter into the courtyard. Applause echoed from inside. The auction must've started.

She turned toward the sound, then glanced back at him. "I need to go back inside."

"I don't want to say goodbye," he blurted.

Her eyes narrowed just slightly, her tone careful. "Well, you're welcome to stay. You can always bid on something."

He caught the faintest flicker of emotion behind her composure. Hesitation, maybe, or hope before she turned toward the noise.

He followed her inside, not sure what to expect but unwilling to give up.

The ballroom buzzed with energy. Applause rippled through the crowd as a man in a navy suit lifted his paddle, outbidding the last contender for a golf weekend package.

Dante scanned the room, and everywhere he looked, there was Scarlett. Her touch was in everything. The shimmer of frosted greenery on the tables, the soft scent of vanilla and pine, the seamless flow of each reveal. She moved through the crowd like she belonged to it, laughing, charming, steady. Every time someone called her name, she turned with that effortless smile that made people feel like *they* were the reason the night sparkled. But he knew better. This wasn't luck or charm. It was all her.

When the final auction item, a weeklong stay at a Sedona villa, was announced, Scarlett stepped up to the microphone. The room quieted. She adjusted the mic, her voice calm and warm as it filled the space.

"Before we wrap up tonight, I just want to say thank you. Every dollar you've given goes toward giving women and children a safe place to start over. For them, this isn't just a fundraiser. It's hope. A second chance."

She paused, scanning the crowd, and for one heartbeat, her gaze caught his. It was only a moment, but it felt like the air shifted.

"And if there's one thing I've learned," she continued, "it's that second chances don't always look the way we expect. Sometimes they come wrapped in hard lessons and detours, but they're worth holding onto."

Applause rose around her, but Dante barely heard it. His chest ached in a way that had nothing to do with nostalgia. He lifted his glass, a quiet toast meant only for her.

"Here's to second chances," he murmured.

* * *

The last of the applause faded, replaced by the softer sounds of people gathering coats and finishing drinks. Scarlett handed off her clipboard to a volunteer with a tired smile. Her cheeks ached from smiling, her feet throbbed, and her heart...well, that was a different kind of ache.

Everything had gone perfectly. The event exceeded its goal, and the guests glowed with wine and goodwill. By every measure, the night was a success. So why did she feel like she might come apart if she didn't get a minute alone?

She slipped through a side door into the courtyard. Cool air met her, laced with citrus and candle smoke. String lights still glowed above, their reflections dancing on the fountain's surface. For the first time all evening, she let herself breathe.

Dante stood a few yards away, his tie loosened, holding a drink in his hand. He smiled when he saw her.

"Hey," he said softly.

"Hey." She stepped closer, her heart pounding more than she wanted. "We raised a lot of money, so I'll forgive you for sneaking in without an RSVP."

That earned a faint grin. "Would've ruined the surprise. Besides, I doubt you have answered if I tried."

She let out a breath that was half laugh, half sigh. "Probably right."

"You look happy," he said.

Her throat tightened. "I'm... getting there."

He nodded slowly, his gaze steady. "You did an incredible thing tonight."

"Thank you." She hesitated. "It mattered. To all of us."

He looked away, jaw tight, like holding something in. "I didn't come here to make things complicated."

"Then why *did* you?"

He exhaled, a quiet, rueful laugh. "Because staying away didn't work."

Her heart gave an unhelpful jolt.

"I told myself you'd moved on," he said, voice low. "That what happened was too much to come back from. But I couldn't take it anymore, Scarlett. I can't stand not being with you." He hesitated, eyes softening.

"Then I saw you tonight, and you look happy. And I realized that's all I ever wanted for you. Even if it isn't with me."

Scarlett stared at him, not sure whether to thank him or tell him he'd just broken her heart all over again.

"That's...nice," she managed, her voice catching. "But it doesn't change what happened."

He nodded once. "No. Nothing can. But maybe it's time we talked about it."

Her pulse stumbled. "Kelly?"

He didn't flinch. "Yeah. About Kelly."

Her stomach tightened. For weeks, she'd trained herself not to think about that day. The moment Kelly walked into Eclipse like some ghost from his past, smiling as if she owned the place. Now she had a choice: to hear him out or walk away.

"She showed up without warning," he said, voice low. "I hadn't seen her in over a year. And the things she said—" He stopped, exhaling. "They weren't true. Yes, we dated, but it was never serious."

Scarlett folded her arms, more to steady herself than anything. "You didn't exactly rush to stop her."

"I should have." His tone was quiet, stripped of defense. "I was blindsided. Angry. Stupid. But there's nothing between us."

Something in his voice, the tired, raw, honest tone, hit straight through her defenses. For a moment, she saw not the confident man who'd shattered her heart, but the one who'd spent his life trying to prove he was enough.

"You hurt me," she said softly.

"I know." His voice roughened. "And I hate that I did. So here I am. No excuses. No backup plan."

A shaky laugh escaped her. She blinked fast, refusing to let tears win. "You just let me walk out."

"I called after you," he said quietly. "You didn't hear me."

There was no defensiveness in his voice this time. Just regret.

"I didn't want to believe her," Scarlett whispered. "But it felt so familiar. That moment when you realize you're just temporary. I should have stood there and confronted you, but the feeling was overwhelming."

He stepped closer, brow furrowed. "I never saw you as temporary."

She shook her head, breath trembling. "Doesn't matter how you saw me, Dante. It's how I felt. And that night—" She swallowed hard. "That night I thought I'd fallen for someone who was never really mine."

He went still. "You were wrong."

She wanted to believe him. God, she did. But the sting of humiliation still burned too deep.

"You could've called," she said. "You could've explained."

"I tried." His mouth lifted in a rueful smile. "Half a dozen times. Every message sounded wrong. I figured you'd block my number before I got it right."

That earned the faintest flicker of a smile. "You weren't wrong."

He chuckled softly. "Figures."

The silence that followed wasn't heavy anymore. It just... lingered.

Scarlett looked down, then back up. "So, what now? You came back to clear your conscience?"

"No," he said. "I came back because I love you. And I can't stop thinking about what I lost."

Butterflies skittered through her stomach as she processed what he'd said. "You love me?"

"Yes," he said, steady and sure. "I do."

The words hit harder than she expected. For a second, something in her wanted to believe him. Wanted to let the ache in her chest soften. But then came the memory she couldn't shake: Kelly's smug smile, the whispers, the humiliation that had left her standing there, exposed.

She swallowed hard. "You don't get to fix this with words, Dante."

His expression didn't change, but his eyes did—something weary, almost broken. "I know. I just needed you to hear them."

Scarlett drew in a slow breath. Her throat burned, but she forced her voice to stay steady. "Well... you've said them. Good night, Dante." Without another word, she turned and walked away.

Would she always run away if she thought someone was cheating on her? Could she ever trust again? She needed time alone to think about what she really wanted.

Chapter 28

For three nights, sleep hadn't stuck. Every time Dante closed his eyes, his mind kicked into overdrive—Scarlett, his dad, the restaurant, all of it on repeat. He'd screwed up everything that mattered. Lost the girl. Let his old man down. Even the dream he'd spent his life chasing didn't look worth it anymore.

By two a.m., he gave up. Threw on a pair of jeans. Grabbed his keys and left the hotel. He told himself he was just taking a drive. Just getting some fresh air. But the truth was, his car always seemed to end up at the same destination. Eclipse Lounge. The restaurant was the one place that still made sense, even when nothing else did.

When he turned into the parking lot, the first thing he noticed was the smoke. Thin and gray, drifting up from the kitchen vent. He parked and opened the driver's side door. When he did, the smell came. Burned oil, electrical wire, and something worse.

"Ah, hell."

He called 911 and ran toward the door.

The side entrance was cracked open, and smoke poured out in thick, rolling clouds. Somewhere inside, someone was coughing.

"Hello?" he shouted.

A faint panicked voice answered. "Help! I can't—"

The voice sounded like it came from the storage room. He grabbed a rag from the supply cart, wrapped it over his mouth, and pushed through the haze. The kitchen was already a furnace. Flames climbed the wall near the stove, licking at the cabinets. He dropped low, half-blind, calling out again until he found her. Lena, one of the night cleaners, huddled behind a rack, frozen in terror.

"Come on," he said, pulling her up and wrapping his jacket over her. "Stay low. We're going out the side door."

She coughed hard, trembling. "I can't see."

"I've got you."

He guided her forward, one arm around her shoulders, keeping her moving through the smoke. The heat seared the back of his neck and scalded his arm, but they made it to the door just as a burst of flame hit the ceiling.

They stumbled outside, both coughing hard, collapsing onto the asphalt. Lena sobbed, clutching his jacket. "You...you came through the smoke for me, Mr. Rivera."

"Yeah," he rasped, catching his breath. "Couldn't let you clean up that mess alone."

She let out a weak laugh that turned into a cough.

Sirens wailed in the distance, growing louder. The adrenaline began to fade, replaced by the sharp burn of his arm where his sleeve had melted against his skin. When the firefighters arrived, they pulled a medic toward him, but Dante waved them off. "She needs it more."

He stood there, chest heaving, watching the flames die under the steady spray of water. The restaurant he'd poured months into looked bruised, blackened—but still standing.

And somehow, so was he.

The paramedic returned. Those burns look bad. You need to have them looked at."

"Okay."

He reached into his pocket for his phone, hesitated, then put his phone back in his pocket. He'd call his father from the hospital.

* * *

Ribet, Ribet, Ribet.

Scarlett opened her eyes, confused, until she realized the steady frog croak was coming from her cell phone. Recognizing Rayna's ring, she reached across the bed to her nightstand and grabbed the phone. "What's up?"

"Are you watching the news?" Rayna's voice came out breathless.

"No, I'm not even up yet. Why?"

"The Eclipse Lounge is on fire."

Scarlett shot straight up in bed. "What? When?"

Earlier this morning. The reporter said it was electrical, but—" Rayna hesitated. "Dante pulled someone out before the fire department arrived. One of the cleaning crew. They're calling him a hero."

Scarlett's heart lurched. "Were they hurt?"

"Smoke inhalation. Burns. I don't know. He's at the hospital."

Before Rayna could say another word, Scarlett threw back the covers and reached for her clothes, her pulse already racing.

"I'll call you back."

"Scarlett—"

But she'd already disconnected the call.

She was out the door in minutes, keys in hand, hair still damp from the world's fastest shower. Her mind replayed Rayna's words in an endless loop. *Dante pulled someone out of the fire. At the hospital.*

The drive across town blurred. Stoplights, traffic, all in the background. Her fingers clenched the steering wheel so tightly her knuckles ached. She told herself she was just checking that everyone was okay. That's all.

But when she turned into the hospital parking lot, parked, and climbed out, her pulse was hammering in her ears. She dashed through the entrance and was headed to the information station when she saw him.

Dante stood near the elevation talking with a nurse, his dark hair tousled, a streak of soot still along his jaw. His sleeve was torn, his arm bandaged from wrist to elbow.

She started toward him before she could think, calling his name. "Dante!"

He turned, and for a split second, surprise flickered across his face. "Scarlett," he said, voice raspy, tired.

She stopped a few feet away, breath catching. "You're okay?"

"Mostly." He gave a grin. "A few burns. Smoke inhalation. They said I'm lucky."

Her voice broke. "Lucky? You ran into a fire!"

He shrugged, wincing a little. "Someone had to get her out."

Scarlett shook her head, frustration and fear colliding. "You could've been killed, Dante."

"Could've," he said quietly. "But I wasn't."

For a moment, neither of them moved, then she ran to him and threw her arms around his neck.

He winced. "Careful, my neck's blistered."

"Oh, I'm sorry." She removed her arms from him.

"It's okay. Thanks for checking on me."
He brushed a strand of hair from her cheek.
"I'm not going anywhere, Scarlett." He
looked her straight in the eye. "I mean it."

She rolled her eyes at him and backed
away slightly. "Well, I'm glad you're all right.
Do you need a ride?"

"Drop me off at the Eclipse, if you don't
mind."

"Not a problem."

The drive from the hospital to the
restaurant was quiet. Neither of them spoke
much. But when she turned onto the street
and saw the yellow caution tape and the faint
haze still drifting above the roofline, her
chest tightened.

Eclipse looked wounded. The front
doors were propped open, fans running to
air out the smoke. A few workers carried
boxes of supplies to a truck, their
movements careful over the debris.

"Oh, Dante, I'm sorry." She parked and
turned to him.

"Yeah, it doesn't look good."

"Do you want me to stick around?"

"No. Nothing you can do. I need to make
a few calls. My dad, insurance, let the staff
know they're out of a job for a few days,
maybe weeks. Who knows?"

She nodded. "Call if you need anything,"

Her heart hurt for him as she watched
him walk toward the building. He looked
wrecked—physically, emotionally—but alive.

"He'll be fine," she whispered to herself. But the words didn't settle anything. He could've been killed. The thought made her chest tighten all over again.

For weeks, she'd told herself what happened between them was final. That she'd seen who he really was, and she wasn't going back. Then she remembered how he'd told her that he wasn't going anywhere. Maybe he meant it. Maybe he didn't. But for the first time in a long time, she realized she wanted to find out.

Chapter 29

The next morning, sunlight streamed through the blinds, far too bright for how little she'd slept. Scarlett pulled a pillow over her face and groaned. Her throat felt tight, her mind replaying every word from the day before.

By seven, she'd given up on pretending she could ignore it. She showered, threw her hair into a messy bun, and was about to head to her office when her phone rang. It was Rebecca.

"Good morning," her friend's voice sounded bright for so early. "Would you have time to go with me to the shelter this morning. I'm cleaning and have some donations to drop off. Mick won't let me go by myself anymore. So annoying."

"Well, I don't blame him. I'll head right over."

An hour later, they were driving toward the shelter, the back seat loaded with a bag full of clothes and bedding.

"I heard all about Dante. He's quite the guy." Rebecca said.

"He's fine. Everyone's fine."

"Mmhmm." Rebecca crossed her arms over her belly. "And you just happened to check for yourself."

"I heard he got hurt," Scarlett said defensively. "I had to check on him."

"You did what anyone would do if they still cared."

"I don't." The words came too fast, too sharp. Her grip tightened on the steering wheel. "At least, I don't want to."

Rebecca tilted her head. "Then why do you look like you've been hit by a truck named Regret?"

Scarlett huffed out a small laugh, shaking her head. "Because I'm an idiot. Because I spent weeks convincing myself he was this selfish, thoughtless man who didn't deserve another chance. And then he goes and pulls someone out of a burning building."

"That doesn't erase what happened."

"I know. But it's harder to stay angry when you realize you still care whether he's breathing."

Rebecca was quiet for a long moment. Then she said gently, "Maybe that's the point, Scar. Caring doesn't mean you forgive him. It just means you're still human."

Scarlett exhaled slowly, eyes burning. "I hate when you sound reasonable."

"It's a curse."

They both laughed, and for a fleeting moment, the heaviness in Scarlett's chest eased.

When they reached the shelter, it was already buzzing with activity. Volunteers sorted donations, kids chased each other around the tables, and somewhere in the kitchen, someone was burning toast.

Scarlett stood by the front office window, waiting for Rebecca. She was dropping off her donations and chatting about who would do what while she was on maternity leave.

Through the window, she spotted him. Dante stood near the back of Joe's truck, sleeves rolled, lifting a crate of canned goods and cleaning supplies from the bed. He looked tired, his arm still bandaged from the fire, but he was smiling as he talked with one of the volunteers.

She drew a slow breath and stepped outside.

When he saw her, his smile widened. "Hey."

"Hey, yourself." She stopped a few feet away, folding her arms. "What brings you here?"

"The supplier I use for the restaurant had extras. Since Eclipse is out of business for the time being, I figured the shelter could use them."

"That's thoughtful."

He shrugged. "They do good work here. I wanted to help."

Scarlett studied him. There was no hint of charm in his voice, none of the practiced confidence she used to brace herself against. Just quiet sincerity.

"You shouldn't be lifting anything," she said, noticing the bandage still on his arm.

"Funny," he murmured, "the nurse said that yesterday too."

Her mouth twitched. "You don't listen very well, do you?"

He just laughed.

Two of the women volunteers walked up. "Mr. Rivera, what can we help you with?"

"There are some smaller boxes. You can take those. I'll get the bigger ones," Dante said, already moving to grab them.

Scarlett followed without thinking, watching as he carried box after box, careful with the kids running around, patient with every question. He didn't once look at her for approval.

When the last box was stacked, she found herself saying quietly, "You didn't have to do all this."

"I know," he said again. "But I wanted to."

She hesitated, then sighed. "You should probably head home. You still look half-dead."

He grinned faintly. "You always did know how to flatter a guy."

Scarlett rolled her eyes, but the corner of her mouth curved despite herself. "Go. Before I put you to work for real."

Dante went toward the door. But just before stepping outside, he paused. "What are you doing for dinner tonight?"

Scarlett's breath caught. It took her a second to respond. she should've told him she was too busy, that she had plans, that she wasn't ready. Instead, she'd heard herself say, "Dinner's fine."

* * *

Dante pulled the car into the parking lot of a little Italian restaurant on Main. He glanced at her. "I've heard good reviews about this place. I've been wanting to try it."

"Sounds good to me."

Warm scents of freshly baked bread, tomato sauce, meatballs, melted cheese, and other delicious aromas hit the moment they stepped through the door. He'd made a reservation, so they were seated immediately.

"Smells wonderful in here."

"That's always a good sign," he smiled. "What are you having?"

She studied the menu, "Penne with marinara sauce."

"Okay." He scanned the list of options. "I'll go with Mama's Favorite Lasagna." He chuckled. "Hope mama knows how to cook."

"Behave, besides, no one cooks as good as you do."

He smiled. "You're prejudiced. And I'm learning to manage my expectations."

The waiter appeared with water and a breadbasket. They ordered cocktails and, since they already knew what they wanted, ordered their dinner preferences as well.

"I picked this place because they don't do pretentious," he said. "And because I was hoping to bribe you with pasta."

"Smart strategy."

"Desperate one," he admitted, grinning. His grin faltered into something more serious. "I meant what I said before, Scarlett. I'm not asking you to forget. I want to start again. No drama, no half-truths."

She held his gaze for a long moment. "You're really bad at casual conversation."

"I'm really bad at pretending," he said quietly.

Scarlett leaned back, exhaling. "Then don't. Just be here. That's all I want tonight."

The server returned with his whiskey and her lemon drop martini.

He took her hand and lightly squeezed it. "I can do that."

She nodded. They both took a sip of their drink.

When the food came, they ate and talked about everything *except* what had happened between them. Scarlett told him about her new project; he told her about rebuilding Eclipse and how his father, shockingly, had offered to invest again.

The rest of the evening flowed easily. By dessert, he'd made her laugh. Not the careful, polite kind, but real laughter. The kind he'd missed.

When they walked out to the parking lot, the night was chilly, the air scented with rain and lemon from the restaurant's trees.

The drive back to Scarlett's place was quiet, but not uncomfortable. The kind of quiet that hummed with everything unspoken. Streetlights swept across her profile—soft, calm, beautiful in a way that made his chest ache.

When they pulled into her driveway and stopped, she didn't move right away.

"Do you want to come in?" she asked, voice low.

Dante's heart kicked once, hard. "If you're sure."

"I'm sure."

Inside, the house smelled slightly like vanilla and cinnamon. The faint glow from the kitchen light spilled into the living room. Scarlett slipped off her heels, setting them neatly by the door, then turned toward him.

He didn't reach for her right away. He just looked, really looked at the woman who'd challenged him, forgiven him just enough to let him try again.

"I meant what I said at dinner," he said quietly. "I don't want to mess this up again."

She stepped closer, her voice steady. "Then don't."

He lifted a hand to her cheek, thumb brushing her skin. She leaned into his touch, eyes closing for a heartbeat. Then she rose on her toes and kissed him. Slow at first, careful, like they were both remembering how.

The kiss deepened, but it wasn't about fire this time. It was relief. Forgiveness. The simple truth that they'd both stopped running.

When they finally pulled apart, she rested her forehead against his chest, breathing him in. "You're staying, right?"

He smiled, pressing his lips to her hair. "Yeah. I'm not going anywhere."

Chapter 30

The rich aroma of coffee coaxed Scarlett from a deep, dream-induced sleep. She stretched an arm across the bed, fingertips brushing cool sheets where Dante should've been. For one dizzy second, she wondered if last night could have been only a wonderful dream. Then came the unmistakable clatter of pots and pans from the kitchen, followed by a muffled curse that made her smile.

Not a dream after all. Grinning, she pushed back the covers and stood. Dante's shirt was crumpled on the floor next to her feet. She picked it up and, feeling the impulse, tugged it on. Then she headed out to investigate whatever culinary masterpiece he thought he was creating.

She padded barefoot down the hall, and when she reached the kitchen doorway, she stopped and had to bite back a laugh. Dante stood in front of her open refrigerator, hair rumpled, wearing nothing but blue boxer shorts and confusion. A carton of almond milk dangled from his hand like it had personally offended him.

"Where's your food?" he said, his deep voice still rough from sleep.

Scarlett leaned against the doorframe, amused. "I guess I haven't been to the grocery store lately."

He turned, grinning when he saw her wearing his shirt. "I'm not giving up," he said as he opened the pantry and stared inside. "You've got... crackers, peanut butter, and... is this instant oatmeal from 2019?"

She laughed. "Vintage. Adds flavor."

He closed the pantry and gave her a sexy grin that made her pulse skip. "You really don't cook, do you?"

"Not unless you count ordering takeout."

He smiled, crossed the room, kissed her cheek, and then poured her a cup of coffee. "Good thing I do," he murmured as he handed her the cup.

Scarlett accepted it, smiling over the rim. "So, what's for breakfast, Chef?"

He leaned close enough for her to feel his breath. "You tell me. You're the one who invited me to stay."

Scarlett opened her mouth to reply, something clever, maybe a little flirtatious, but before she could, her phone buzzed across the counter, vibrating against the granite like it was possessed.

She frowned. "Who's calling this early?"

Dante gave a grin. "Probably someone who knows you don't cook."

Scarlett rolled her eyes and snatched the phone. The screen flashed Rayna. She sighed and accepted, putting it on speaker so she could drink her coffee.

"Scarlett!" Rayna's voice shrieked so loudly that Dante turned. "She's in labor!"

"What?" Scarlett blinked. "Rayna, slow down. What's going on?"

"Rebecca! Her water broke like twenty minutes ago. We're on the way to the hospital, and she's yelling at Mick for driving too slow, and I think she just threw a shoe at him."

Scarlett nearly choked on her coffee. "Oh my gosh. Wait, *now*? But she's not due for another two weeks."

"Tell that to the screaming woman in the passenger seat," Rayna shouted. "Meet us at the hospital. And hurry." The line went dead.

Scarlett stared at her phone, still processing. "Rebecca's in labor."

Dante blinked. "I sort of gathered that."

"I have to go!" She spun toward the bedroom, half laughing, half panicking.

He followed, amused. "I'm coming with you."

"You'd better get dressed fast," she called over her shoulder, already grabbing her purse.

"Uh, I'll meet you. I need a shower. And a shirt."

By the time Scarlett pulled into the hospital parking lot, she was still wearing Dante's shirt under her jacket and had one tennis shoe untied. Her phone kept buzzing with messages from Rayna, each one more frantic than the last.

Where are you??

We're in maternity! She's threatening to bite Mick!

Bring snacks!!

Scarlett sprinted through the hospital's sliding doors. She spotted Rayna instantly — a blur of curls and panic —running toward her from the elevator.

"There you are," Rayna stated, grabbing Scarlett's arm. "She's already at eight centimeters. Mick looks like he's about to pass out, and Rebecca keeps yelling that he's never touching her again."

Scarlett blinked. "Wow. Romantic."

"It's like a live-action horror movie," Rayna said, leading her toward the maternity ward. "Only with more screaming and less popcorn."

When they reached the maternity waiting area, Rebecca's dad sat slumped in a chair, pale and wide-eyed, clutching a hospital bag like a life raft.

"I'll tell Rebecca you're here. You get checked in as a friend," Rayna told her.

When Rayna opened the double doorway, Rebecca's unmistakable voice could be heard demanding ice chips and threatening bodily harm in the same breath.

Scarlett gave her information to the woman at the front desk, then crossed the waiting room to where Mr. Prentice sat, elbows on his knees, a cup of coffee cooling beside him. She eased into the chair next to him and gently squeezed his arm.

"How's she doing?"

He gave a helpless shrug. "As good as anyone in her position, I guess. She's loud enough."

Scarlett smiled despite the nerves fluttering in her chest. "That sounds about right."

"She wants you here," he said quietly. "Said it wouldn't feel real until her girlfriends showed up."

Her throat tightened. "We're here now."

A moment later, Rayna appeared, breathless but smiling. "Your turn. I'll wait here with Gramps."

Scarlett stood quickly. "Thanks." She hurried toward Rebecca's room, heart pounding.

The next hour passed in a blur of laughter, ice chips, and shoulder rubs as the girls took turns comforting the mom-to-be, doing whatever they could to help.

When it was finally Rayna's turn again, an exhausted Scarlett slipped back into the waiting area. She sank into a chair beside Mr. Prentice, both of them pretending to read magazines, though neither could focus on the words. The low hum of hospital sounds filled the silence between them, carrying the soft echoes of Rebecca's voice from down the hall.

Ten minutes later, the double doors swung open, and a nurse gently ushered out Rayna. "She only wants her husband and her mother," the nurse said firmly before disappearing back inside.

Rayna stumbled into the hall, looking half-insulted, half-relieved. "Apparently, I was *too* helpful," she huffed, smoothing her blouse. "Mick's in there. Poor guy looked greener than the walls."

Scarlett bit back a laugh. "You got kicked out of the delivery room?"

"I was just trying to remind Rebecca to breathe. You'd think I was storming the castle."

"Sit," Scarlett said, grinning. "She's in good hands."

Rayna plopped down beside her, shooting Mr. Prentice a polite smile before sighing in defeat.

"What were you doing at Rebecca's this early?" Scarlett asked.

"I wasn't," Rayna said, shaking her head. "I was at Mo's helping Mick with the schedule. Rebecca called, Mick panicked, so I rode along to keep him calm while he picked her up."

Scarlett smiled. "Smart move."

Rayna gave a tired grin. "Yeah, until they kicked me out of the action."

Just then, Scarlett's phone buzzed on her lap. She glanced down, and her pulse jumped when she saw the name. Dante.

On my way. Don't panic.

Scarlett smiled to herself, shaking her head. "Too late," she murmured.

Rayna arched a brow. "What?"

"Nothing," Scarlett said quickly, unable to hide her grin. "Backup's on the way."

A few minutes later, the elevator dinged, and Dante walked toward her. His hair appeared slightly damp from a quick shower, and jeans and a fitted T-shirt replaced the clothes he'd worn last night. He carried a carton holding coffee cups and a brown paper bag that smelled suspiciously like bakery heaven.

"You made it," Scarlett said, relief softening her voice.

He handed her one of the cups. "Hazelnut latte. And chocolate croissants." He held out the paper bag.

She accepted it with a grateful sigh. "You're officially my hero."

"Yeah, mine too," Rayna said, eying the bag of bakery goods. "I call dibs on anything with frosting."

Dante laughed and passed her a napkin. "I think we can manage that."

Scarlett introduced Dante to Mr. Prentice. He offered him a croissant, but it was graciously declined.

After a moment of silence, he leaned closer and whispered, "That shirt looks better on you than it does on me."

Her cheeks warmed. She'd forgotten what she was wearing when she ran out of the house. She'd shimmied into the first pair of jeans in her closet, grabbed shoes, a coat, and ran. She pulled her jacket tighter to hide what she had on underneath it, then met his gaze. "I'll take that as a compliment."

"It was one."

Rayna cleared her throat pointedly, tearing into a croissant. "You two want me to give you a minute, or can we just collectively stress-eat our way through this labor?"

From his seat beside Scarlett, Dante tried not to stare, but she made it impossible. Her hair was a little wild, her jacket pulled tight against her body, and yet she still looked beautiful.

The smell of coffee and disinfectants hung in the air, grounding Dante in the strange mix of nerves and anticipation that filled the waiting room.

He glanced toward Scarlett again. She was trying to look calm, but her foot tapped a restless rhythm on the tile.

"You okay?" he asked softly.

She nodded, managing a small smile. "Just ready for the baby."

Before he could reply, the double doors at the end of the hall opened. Mick stepped out, scrubs wrinkled, hair flattened on one side, and wearing the biggest grin Dante had ever seen.

"She's here," Mick said, his voice rough with emotion. "We've got a healthy baby girl."

Scarlett shot to her feet, her hand flying to her mouth. "Oh my gosh."

"Both doing great," Mick said, still grinning. "Olivia's with them, and now she wants her dad."

Rebecca's dad stood so fast his chair nearly tipped. "That's me," he said, brushing at his eyes before following Mick down the hall.

Rayna let out a half-laugh, half-sob and turned to Scarlett. "A girl."

Scarlett nodded, tears spilling freely. "We have a girl."

They reached for each other, laughing and crying together as they hugged tightly.

Dante watched, smiling.

When the girls finally pulled apart, Scarlett wiped her cheeks and shrugged. "I'm a disaster."

Dante handed her a napkin. "Yeah," he said gently, "but a beautiful one."

She shot him a watery smile, and somehow, in that fluorescent waiting room, everything felt exactly as it should.

The three of them sat for a while in the quiet hum of hospital sounds. Nurses passed, machines beeped, and the faint echo of newborn cries drifted from another wing. Scarlett leaned back, her head resting against his shoulder.

A few minutes later, a nurse poked her head into the waiting room. "You can come back now."

Rayna grabbed Scarlett's hand before the words finished leaving the nurse's mouth. "That's us," she said.

Dante watched them hurry down the hall. He followed a few steps behind, stopping in the doorway as they slipped into the room.

Rebecca was propped against a stack of pillows, blonde hair a tangled mess, cheeks flushed. Mick stood beside her, cradling a tiny pink bundle.

"Hey," Rebecca said, her voice rough but glowing. "Meet Miss Harper Lynn Prentice."

Scarlett gasped, pressing a hand to her heart. "She's beautiful."

Rayna leaned in, instantly crying again. "Oh, look at her little nose. I'm done. I'm just done."

Mick chuckled softly. "She's got her mom's lungs. Did you hear her earlier?"

Rebecca gave him a teasing smile. "You're lucky I can't reach the ice chips."

The room was filled with laughter. Dante lingered by the door, watching the women crowd around the new family, their voices dropping to soft coos and whispers.

He didn't belong in the middle of it, but he didn't want to leave either. His chest tightened. He wasn't sure what that feeling was, hope, maybe. Or the realization that this messy, loud, beautiful moment was exactly the kind of life he'd been missing.

When Scarlett finally turned toward him, her smile reached her eyes. "Come meet her," she said tenderly.

He stepped closer, the tiny bundle barely visible beneath a pink blanket. The baby's fingers flexed once, impossibly small, and a sound caught in his throat before he could stop it.

"She's... perfect," he said quietly.

Rebecca smiled. "That's what we think too."

Just then, the door opened, and Trisha peeked in, holding a vase of pink and white carnations. "Sorry, I'm late. We had a horse to load, and he wouldn't cooperate."

"You're right on time." Rebecca waved her in. "Come here and see the baby."

As Trisha stepped inside, Dante took it as his cue to leave. He caught Scarlett's gaze and gave her a nod toward the door and mouthed that he'd wait for her. Then he slipped out quietly, the sound of happy laughter lingering behind him.

Dante found his way back to the waiting area, the air cooler and quieter out there. The adrenaline and emotion of the delivery room still clung to him, a strange mix of joy and something he didn't quite have words for.

He sank into one of the chairs and stared at the coffee cup still sitting on the table from earlier. A baby. A family. The way Rebecca looked at Mick, tired but overflowing with love, stirred something in him.

He'd spent years chasing the next kitchen, the next menu, the next approval from his father. But sitting here, surrounded by vending machines and baby cries echoing from down the hall, maybe he'd been chasing the wrong things.

The double doors opened. Scarlett walked toward him. She was tearstained but smiling, her eyes still bright from the emotion of it all.

"Hey," he said.

"Hey," she echoed as she sank into the chair beside his.

"She's beautiful," Scarlett whispered.

He nodded. "Yeah. She really is."

For a moment, neither of them spoke. Then Scarlett let out a soft, almost disbelieving laugh. "Rebecca's a mom. That still feels wild to say."

"Yeah," Dante said, glancing over at her. "You'll make a good one someday."

Her breath caught slightly, but she smiled. "That's a long way off."

"Doesn't mean I can't picture it."

Scarlett gave him an unreadable look.

For a while, they sat in the waiting room, the sounds of newborn cries and distant laughter drifting down the hall. Scarlett flipped through a magazine while Dante leaned forward, elbows on his knees.

Finally, she tossed the magazine down. "I don't think they'll miss us if we leave."

"Whenever you're ready."

By the time they left the hospital, the December sun was low, streaking the sky in shades of rose and gold. The air carried a crisp chill. In the parking lot, their breath clouded faintly as they walked side by side, Scarlett jingling her keys, as they glanced around the rows of vehicles.

"It's been quite a day," she said softly.

Dante nodded. "Yeah. Sure has."

They stopped at her car first. His vehicle was parked two spaces away. She shifted her purse to one shoulder. "I'm going to swing by the shops on Main before heading home. Need to grab a few last-minute Christmas things."

"Speaking of Christmas, do you have plans?"

"Not much. I'm keeping it low-key this year. My parents are on a cruise with their friends."

He smiled faintly. "My mom's already planning a dinner that could feed half of Manhattan, and my dad's pretending everything's perfect while quietly judging the menu."

Scarlett tilted her head. "That sounds... complicated."

He gave a short laugh, rubbing the back of his neck. "That's one word for it. My mom loves any excuse to get the family together. My dad—he's harder to read."

Her voice softened. "I'm sure he loves you."

"Yeah," Dante admitted quietly. "I've spent years trying to make him proud. Building Eclipse Lounge... that was me proving I could stand on my own." He paused, his gaze finding hers. "I thought success would make me happy. But lately, it feels like my life's meant to go in a different direction."

Scarlett's brow lifted slightly. "Dante..."

He took a step closer, pulse hammering. Before he could second-guess himself, he reached for her hand. Her fingers felt small in his. "Come with me to New York," he said. "Spend Christmas with me and my family."

Her eyes widened, and he could practically feel the question hang in the air between them. *Too much? Too soon?*

"Are you serious?" she asked.

"Completely." A slow smile tugged at his mouth. "It's last-minute and probably chaotic, but I want them to meet the woman who's been driving me crazy for weeks."

Her breath hitched. "You really want me to come with you?" she asked softly.

"Yes," he said, voice low and steady. "They'll love you." His chest tightened as he added, "I already do."

Scarlett's eyes widened slightly. Seconds passed. He watched her weigh his request, thinking about what he'd said. Then she took a quiet breath and asked, "You love me?"

"I do, Scarlett."

"I love you too, Dante. I think I have since the first time I saw you at Lazy Jake's. I just had to get over my trust issues."

For a beat, he just stared at her, not quite believing he'd heard her right. Then a grin broke across his face, slow and unstoppable. "I thought I'd never hear those words."

She laughed. "And I'll go to New York with you."

He grabbed her in a hug that lifted her feet off the ground. "Best Christmas gift I could ask for."

Scarlett's smile deepened. "You haven't opened any gifts yet."

He chuckled, still holding her hand. "Pretty sure I just did."

She laughed. Then she gasped. "Oh, my God. I don't have anything to wear."

"Good thing that's a mall right down the street."

Chapter 31

Snow drifted in lazy spirals under the glow of the porch light as Scarlett stepped out of the cab and looked toward the Rivera home. Her breath caught. Even from the sidewalk, the home radiated luxury. A pair of evergreen trees sat on each side of the entryway, draped in white lights, and a massive wreath with a red bow hung on the door.

Beside her, Dante smiled as he reached for their luggage. "Mom goes a little overboard this time of year, so be prepared."

Before Scarlett could reply, the front door flew open. A petite woman with dark hair and an apron that read *Mrs. Claus in Training* hurried down the steps.

"Dante!" she cried, arms open wide. "Welcome home."

Dante grinned, setting down the bags just in time to catch his mother in a hug. "Hi, Mom."

Then she turned to Scarlett, her eyes lighting up. "You must be Scarlett. Oh, honey, look at you. You're gorgeous."

"Thank you, Mrs. Rivera. It's so nice to—"

"Oh, please," the woman said, waving a dismissive hand. "It's Elena." She looped her arm through Scarlett's. "Come inside before you freeze. I've got hot cider, too many cookies, and a husband pretending to hate Christmas music."

"Some things never change." Dante chuckled as he followed behind.

She stepped inside and inhaled the sweetness and tang of vanilla and spice. She glanced around at all the decorations. Strands of garland draped the banister, and candles flickered on every table. In the corner, a towering Douglas Fir tree stood beside the fireplace, perfectly placed glass ornaments sparkling in the firelight, hanging from every branch. She paused for a second, just taking it all in.

Dante leaned close, his voice low near her ear. "You okay so far?"

She nodded slowly, her heart full. "Yeah. It's amazing."

He smiled, his hand brushing hers for a fleeting moment. "Welcome to my world."

Elena bustled ahead of them toward the kitchen, calling over her shoulder, "Make yourselves at home. Dinner's almost ready, and I'll need someone to taste-test my truffle mashed potatoes."

"Grab a seat." Dante pointed to a cream-colored circular sofa. "I'll run our luggage upstairs."

Scarlett nodded. As soon as he headed up the stairs, she eased onto the sofa, then sat quietly, still trying to absorb the scene. All the ornaments sparkling, the sound of classical Christmas music in the background, the warmth that filled every inch of the Rivera home. It must have been wonderful growing up in such a beautiful house, completely different from her modest Arizona ranch-style home.

Dante returned and plopped down next to her. "I'll show you your room later. I think you'll be comfortable."

"I'm sure I will."

"Looks like my son made it." The deep voice came from the archway behind them.

Dante turned. "Hey, Dad." He stood and offered his hand to help her to her feet.

Mr. Rivera stepped into the room. His presence was commanding without trying. His dark hair graying at the temples, his expression a careful balance between pride and distance. "And you must be Scarlett." He held out his hand.

She smiled and took it, hoping her handshake didn't feel as nervous as she felt. "It's so nice to meet you, Mr. Rivera. Your home is beautiful."

He nodded. "Thank you. My wife has an eye for these things." His gaze turned to his son. "I'm glad you decided to be here. We weren't sure if business would keep you out west for the holidays."

Dante's tone stayed even. "I couldn't disappoint mom."

Elena walked toward them, carrying a tray of cider mugs. "Oh, for heaven's sake, it's Christmas, not a board meeting," she scolded lightly, setting down the tray.

The tension broke, replaced by laughter as she handed Scarlett a mug. "Here, sweetheart. Cinnamon stick and a dash of orange. It's practically a hug in a cup."

Scarlett smiled, grateful for the warmth of both the cider and the moment. "It's wonderful, thank you."

Dante glanced at her. The tightness in his shoulders is beginning to relax.

Mr. Rivera studied them both for a beat longer, then cleared his throat. "Dinner in fifteen. Dante, I could use your help carving the roast."

"Lead the way, Dad," Dante replied.

As the two disappeared into the dining room, Elena leaned in and whispered conspiratorially, "Don't let him scare you, dear. He's just allergic to feelings."

Scarlett smiled, her nerves settling. Whatever this Christmas held, she already knew one thing: she'd found love and she was exactly where she was meant to be.

* * *

Dinner had begun. As usual, the Rivera dining room shimmered in soft candlelight, flickering over crystal glassware, and the scent of rosemary and prime rib. His mother was radiant, laughing easily at something Scarlett said, while his dad looked relaxed, even amused.

Dante sat back, letting the comfort of it sink in. This Christmas will be special, he thought as he glanced toward Scarlett. She looked beautiful. She'd changed into a soft red dress that outlined her lovely shape. Her hair was brushed into a stylish updo, her makeup soft and natural. His heart melted as he gazed at her.

The doorbell rang.

His mother paused mid-sentence. "Who could that be?"

Julian frowned, setting down his wine. "We're not expecting anyone, are we?"

Elena pushed back her chair. "Everyone, stay seated. I'll get it."

Her heels clicked across the marble floor, disappearing into the entryway. A beat of silence followed, then the sound of the front door opening. And then—

She screamed.

The sound hit Dante square in the chest. He was on his feet before he knew it, heart pounding as he raced to see what was going on. He reached her, ready for action, only to hear her let out a sound somewhere between a sob and a laugh.

"*Mi hijo...*"

His father rushed to her side.

"Julian. It's our son," she choked out.

In the doorway stood his brother, Dominic, older than he remembered but still tall and broad-shouldered. Now his hair was touched with gray at his temples, like their father's. Beside him, his wife and a young woman, maybe eighteen, with his same dark eyes. A small boy, maybe aged five or six, gripped his mother's hand.

For a moment, the entire room fell silent. It had been nearly nineteen years since Dominic stormed out of the house. Dante remembered the night clearly. The teenage pregnancy confession. His father's anger. The yelling. The door slamming. Dominic had walked away from a college scholarship and a future in the family business, all to be with the woman he loved.

His mother clung to Dominic's arm, laughing and crying all at once.

Dominic smiled, then spoke softly. "Hi, Mom."

His father moved forward slowly, emotion shifting across his face, something Dante couldn't quite name. "You came home," he said quietly.

Dominic nodded. "I should've done it sooner."

"And this must be—"

"You remember, Brittany?" Dominic said.

Both parents nodded.

"Good to see you again, Brittany," his mother replied.

Dominic gestured gently, "And this is our daughter, Lila." He touched Lila's shoulder, then looked at his father. "She wanted to meet her family."

Julian's voice caught slightly. "Lila." He paused for a moment, then he smiled. A real, unpolished smile. "You look just like your grandmother."

"This is Nico, your grandson." Dominic motioned toward the boy.

His mother dabbed at her eyes again, laughing through the tears. "Come in. You must be freezing."

"Yes," his father added, "dinner's on the table."

"We don't want to intrude—"

"Nonsense. You're home. He took the child's hand. "Do you like broccoli?"

Nico made a face. "Yuck."

Jullian laughed, "No? Well, I bet you like chocolate cake." When the child nodded, he added, "We have plenty of cake, too."

Dante caught his brother's eye. As he did, the years between them fell away. "Hey."

Dominic smiled. "Hey, little brother."

And the next thing he knew, the chairs scraped, plates shuffled, and soon the once-formal table was alive with laughter and movement. Brittany helped his mother pass dishes; Lila chatted with Scarlett about New York lights and college plans; Julian whispered something into his grandson's ear, making the boy laugh.

When the table was filled with dishes of food, his father lifted his glass in a toast. "Well," he said, his voice seemed to catch before he found the words. "I didn't think this night could surprise me. But I can't imagine a better one." He looked at Dominic, eyes shining with tears he didn't bother to hide. "Welcome home, son."

Dominic exhaled slowly, emotion flickering across his face. "Thanks, Dad."

The room quieted as they dug into the meal.

Dante paused and reflected on his life. He'd spent years chasing approval. Always trying to prove himself worthy of the Rivera name. But now, sitting here, he knew none of that filled the empty places inside him. This, the noise, the laughter, the forgiveness. For the first time, he didn't feel like he had to earn his place at this table.

He simply belonged.

Scarlett's fingers brushed against his beneath the table. He took her hand, leaned closer, and whispered, "I'm glad you're here."

"I am too."

And Dante realized that, for the first time in years, this house didn't feel cold.

It felt like Christmas.

Epilogue

Six months later.

Scarlett stepped out of the U-Haul and looked toward the single-story stucco house, its pale exterior partly shaded by two newly planted trees. The air smelled faintly of mesquite and citrus, and somewhere down the street, wind chimes played a soft tune.

"This is it," Dante said, stretching as he climbed out of the truck. "Home sweet rental."

She laughed. "That's one way to sell it."

He grinned, walking around to open the back of the U-Haul. "You're the one who picked it."

"Correction," she said, tugging her hair up into a ponytail, "I found it. You're the one who said, 'Let's do it.'"

He handed her a box marked *Kitchen—Fragile*—and grabbed one marked *Misc. Stuff We Probably Don't Need*. "Semantics."

They started up the walkway, arms full, the bright Arizona sun shining down on their shoulders.

At the porch, he balanced his box on one knee and fished in his pants pocket for the keys. "Moment of truth."

The lock clicked, the door groaned, and a wave of cool air rolled out. Scarlett stepped inside first and glanced around. Tile floors, expansive windows, sunlight flooding the empty living room, it smelled like fresh paint and new beginnings.

"You know, I love it already." She carried the box into the kitchen and set it down.

"It's just a rental," he said, stepping in behind her with another box.

"I don't care. It's ours," she countered, smiling.

He placed the box beside hers, straightened, and looked around. "Feels weird," he admitted. "No noise, no chaos."

She glanced over her shoulder. "You're saying that like it's a bad thing."

He chuckled. "Guess I'm just not used to the desert peace and quiet."

They spent the next hour unloading boxes, laughing when she tripped over a rolled-up rug and nearly dropped an entire box of dishes. By the time they collapsed onto the new area rug they'd spread out on the living room floor, the sun had shifted through the windows, casting long stripes of light across the room.

Scarlett stretched out, breathing hard. "I underestimated how much stuff you have."

He chuckled. "You mean *we* have."

She gave him a look. "We? Pretty sure half those boxes are just your coffee mugs."

"Guilty." His lips quirked into a sexy smile.

"So, how much is left to unpack?"

"Just the big stuff. Joe's stopping by later to help with that. Unless you want to tackle it now?"

"Not a chance. Besides, I'm hungry."

"How's pizza sound?"

"Perfect. Did you bring in the cooler yet?"

"By the fridge."

"You order the pizza, I'll get the drinks." She rose from the floor and headed to the kitchen.

Dante placed their order, then stepped into the kitchen beside her. "Dad called earlier. He's sending over the final documents. It's official, the restaurant's mine."

Scarlett smiled, leaning into him. "Congratulations. You earned it."

He kissed her temple. "It feels right this time. Not because I'm trying to prove anything, but because I want to build something that actually matters."

She gave a happy sigh, feeling that truth settle deep inside her. "That's the best reason there is. Hey, we need a celebration. Good thing I put a bottle of champagne in the cooler."

"You think of everything."

"Hello...I am a planner." She opened a box labeled wine glasses and set two on the island's countertop.

"Scarlett," he said softly, his expression thoughtful.

Before she could speak, he dropped to one knee. Her breath caught. "Dante..."

He reached into his pocket, pulled out a small velvet box, and opened it. The large diamond inside sparkled in the slant of afternoon light. "You've been with me through the chaos," he said, voice rough. "You make me want to be better. Not for business, not for my dad, but for us. I don't want to do any of this without you."

Scarlett's vision blurred as tears filled her eyes. "Are you really doing this right now?" she whispered, laughing through the shock.

He smiled, that smile she loved. "I'm doing this right now. Marry me."

For a second, all she could do was stare. The sunlight, the smell of fresh paint, the weight of the moment, it all wrapped around her like something too perfect to be real.

"Yes," she finally breathed, the word trembling out of her. "Yes, of course I'll marry you."

He stood and pulled her into his arms, her laughter muffled against his chest. She could feel his heart pounding, strong and steady. When she looked up into his face, he was smiling so wide it made her laugh again.

"You really know how to make moving day memorable," she teased.

"Just wanted to make sure you'd wear this ring before I unpack all the heavy stuff."

She shook her head, still smiling through tears. "You're impossible."

"Yeah," he said softly, slipping the ring onto her finger. "But I'm yours."

"I love you, Dante."

"I love you, Scarlett."

She leaned against him, her fingers lacing with his. For the first time in a long time, she didn't wonder what came next. She already knew. Every step, every mistake, every second chance had led them right here.

Love, Home. Work. All of it, finally, in the same place.

The End

Dani Petrone is a multi-published author who divides her writing time between her own stories to being half of the Books We Love award-winning team Tia Dani.

Dani resides in Arizona with her fourteen-year-old cat and a senior one-eyed dog. When not writing, you might find her drinking butterscotch martinis with her author friends, playing on social media, or binge-watching suspense movies. She also enjoys touring luxury homes, exploring haunted hot spots, and taking scenic road trips.

Dani's an active member of several writing groups, including a member of The Butterscotch Martini Girls.

Dani Petrone books also published by BWL Publishing
Rebel Heart
Racing for Love